ADVANCE PRAISE FOR TALL TREES

"Frank, poignant and uplifting, *Tall Trees* is a testament to the ability of the human spirit to overcome the pain of abuse. Thomas Paul is here to tell the truth and to remind us that it really can set us free. "

—Sarah Charles Wright, Attorney

"Understanding the reasons why we are the way we are, or do the things we do, is a critical part of our developmental process ..."

"As a psychotherapist for 25 years, I have made this reassurance to many people who have trusted me with being their guide on a very intimate journey. This novel could have been quoted straight from the pages of a therapist's notes. Male survivors of sexual abuse have a voice in Thomas Paul. My hope is by reading this book more survivors will begin the journey of hope, healing and living life without limits."

—Vicki Simmons, LCSW

"Powerful, poignant, and well-written. Wow ... unforgettable."
—Chris Hartman, Fairness Campaign Director

"With a traumatized past and an empowered adulthood, Thomas Paul ignites hope for all survivors of childhood trauma and familial struggles. *Tall Trees* is a must-read for anyone who is passionate about the human condition."

—Carey Moore, LMFT (Licensed Marriage & Family Therapist)

TALL TREES

A Story of Triumph

A Novel

By

Andrea Bouvier

and

Mark Richard Clements

TALL TREES: A STORY OF TRIUMPH

www.talltreesnovel.com

Publisher:
Tall Trees, LLC
PO Box 5036
Louisville, KY 40255-0036
www.talltreesnovel.com
All Rights Reserved

ISBN: 978-0-9856639-0-2 trade paperback
First Edition

Cover Design by Mark Richard Clements

Edited by Peggy DeKay
Interior Layout by Peggy DeKay
peggy@tbowt.com

Bulk Orders

To order additional copies, contact www.talltreesnovel.com, contact page. Quantity discounts are available on bulk purchases of this book for educational and training purposes. Discounts are also available to organizations, associations, libraries, and others. To learn more, contact www.talltreesnovel.com.

To Contact the Authors: markcandandreab@gmail.com

Dedication

From **Andrea Bouvier**

For Sydney and Camryn
—*Strength, Courage, and Love*

To Gary Devon
—*For believing in me*

From **Mark Richard Clements**

For James Emanuel Clements and
June Carol Sengelaub-Clements
—*Rest in Peace*

Introduction

Thomas Paul Stanton was born blessed with a strong personal character, exceptional good looks and, at first glance, appeared to be the all-American dream boy. Born in 1960, at the end of the baby boom, he was raised in a socially revolutionary era of American history. It was the dawning of the age of enlightenment, the sexual revolution, and the fight for individual rights.

Isolated by the obscurity of the burgeoning middle class sprawl, Thomas Paul finds himself standing alone to face unrelenting adversity. With no education, no knowledge of a family life beyond his own, and nowhere to turn, he endures the neglect of his physically and emotionally ill mother, the tyranny of his menacing father, and finally, just as he begins to find new hope, the ultimate abuse and betrayal by a trusted priest.

This is a story about a family, from which hidden pathologies emerged, over time, to form and mold their children into adults and set their moral compasses. It is about parents, and how the environments they create shape us as people of the world.

The writers delve into the heart and mind of Thomas Paul as he, with hope, courage, and deep spiritual convictions, struggles to learn the true meaning of love, forgiveness, and the value in living.

Author Notes

The terms Complex-Post Traumatic Stress Disorder (C-PTSD) and Cognitive Behavioral Therapy (CBT) were terms not yet in use during the historical time frame of this story. The issues faced by Thomas Paul, and the treatment he followed are of historically accurate but would not bear these two medically accurate terms until more recent history.

Through the power of its wealth, the Catholic Church has spent hundreds of millions of dollars forcing thousands of abuse victims into silence by binding them to legal contracts, thereby nullifying the truth of their suffering. The Church now voraciously defends itself on all fronts.

"To the countless children who have been victimized and silenced by the Catholic Church."

—Mark Richard Clements

PART
ONE

"Suffer the misfits."

—Mark Richard Clements

Chapter 1

1963

It was dark. The little boy, now three years old, awoke. He sat up in his baby bed and rubbed his eyes. There was no nightlight, and even the moon failed to cast its usual comforting glow into the room. The townhouse on Fincastle was silent. He shared the small space with his older brother and sisters, but tonight, he couldn't feel their presence. He listened for the sounds of their breathing but all he could hear was his own. He was alone. Afraid. Even at such a young age, he wasn't afraid very often.

He wouldn't cry. He seldom did. Instead, he started rocking back and forth in the tiny, cramped bed. His rhythmic rocking banged the wooden bed slats against the wall, making a loud, repeated thumping sound. He would do this until someone came to check on him.

The bed banged like a shutter in the wind for quite some time before, finally, the door swung open and she came into the room. He could smell her before she reached him: White Shoulders perfume. "Oh, Thomas Paul, my baby. Your daddy and I were next door playing cards. It's okay. I'm here now." She reached for him and he looked up at her. Even in the dim light from the hallway, one could see how pretty she was. Tonight, even though they had only gone next door, she had taken the time to dress up. Petite and stylish, she was a natural blonde but loved wigs and wore them often. Complete with high heels, eyeliner, mascara, and always the perfume, she was movie-star glamorous. He loved to look at her.

She took him in her arms and carried him over to the rocking chair in the corner of the room. They held each other in the stillness. Their mutual adoration and affection were palpable.

"Mommy," he whispered, relieved.

"Did you have a bad dream, honey?" she asked as she stroked his soft, blonde hair.

He didn't answer her. He couldn't. Of course it was *the* dream.

His brother Peter is dragging him along by the arm. Thomas Paul is being pulled faster than his little legs can keep up, and his shoulder is starting to ache from his brother's impatient yanking. Peter is five years older and much stronger.

"Owww! You're hurting me," Thomas Paul whines.

"Tough. If she's gonna make me babysit you, then you gotta do what I say," he says. "I'll let go, but you better keep up with me."

Eyes filled with tears, Thomas Paul rubs his throbbing shoulder socket and watches his brother pull ahead of him and make his way down the street to his friends. His lip quivers. There is nowhere to go. He doesn't like his brother's friends. Some of them are older than Peter, and they play games that he doesn't understand and laugh at things that aren't funny. They sometimes pick on him and he is too little to stand up to them. Still, he can't run away because then his brother might get in trouble for not keeping a close watch on him. If his brother gets punished, he will later turn on Thomas for getting him in trouble.

Thomas Paul hesitates for a moment, then wipes his eyes on his sleeve and hurries to catch up. *It'll be okay.*

In the small common area behind the apartments, some kids have constructed a makeshift tee-pee out of old bed sheets hung over a swing set; it reminds Thomas of a circus tent. He wonders what's inside.

One of Peter's friends comes out of the apartment and spots Thomas Paul.

"Aww, why didja have to bring him? Make him go play in that tent or something." He motions over to the swing set.

Peter looks down at his brother and says, "Yeah, Thomas, you go play over there. I'm going in the house."

"But why? I wanna go with you," Thomas whines.

"No! Just go play by yourself because I don't want you in here."

Resigned to being cast aside by his brother, Thomas sits in the grass for a short while and pouts. It's not long before the uproarious laughter from inside the tent gets the better of his curiosity. He inches up to the gap between the dingy sheets and listens. After looking back towards the apartment one more time, he steps inside.

Above him, a boy hangs by his knees from the bar of the swing set, like an acrobat, with his pants pulled down. His butt is smeared with something gooey and yellowish brown in color. *Why is there mustard on his butt?* Thomas wonders, too young to realize it is feces.

Other boys are laughing and shouting at one another. Thomas doesn't understand why they are laughing. His eyes are wide open as he studies the scene playing out before him. He notices other boys have their pants down too. He feels a hand on his back, pushing him to the ground.

In front of him, a boy stands, holding his penis. A sweaty hand grasps the back of Thomas Paul's neck and forces him to look at the rigid thing, which is inches from his panicked eyes. The boy wiggles it in his face.

"Open your mouth!" someone shouts, giggling.

Out.

Thomas is scared. He doesn't like these games. His heart is pounding in his chest, and he wants to go home. He wants to be with his mom and dad, where he will be safe.

Another hand grabs the back of his head, thrusting it forward. "Open your mouth and put it in!" another barks. More squeals of laughter.

He clamps his lips shut and turns away. *Out!*

Like a trapped animal, he scans the tent for the opening in the sheets, but he is dizzy from the heat and the smell. He can't seem to focus on anything. *Out.* The boys are laughing and pointing at him. There are so many of them. It seems like they have doubled in size and number. *Where is my brother? I want to go home.*

In his baby bed, his eyes dart crazily back and forth behind his eyelids. *Out. Out. Out.* Finally, he is awake, panting. His pillow is damp, and his jaw hurts from clamping it shut in his sleep.

"Shhhh," his mother said rocking. "It was just a dream. You're alright now. It wasn't real. Shhhh."

She didn't know. For the first time in his young life, as she held him gently in her arms, he felt both safe and scared.

Chapter 2

"Horses backs do not curve like this," the teacher snapped. Thomas slid down the back of his chair in silent horror as Mrs. Mullins walked back and forth in front of the class, the soles of her thick black shoes echoing against the wood floor with her slow, deliberate steps. She held up his drawing for all to see. The other kids stared wide-eyed at the innocent, childish picture of the chestnut pony, now half-slaughtered by a cruel, bloodlike arrow, courtesy of a thick, red, felt pen. A few of his peers snickered and Thomas blushed, fighting back tears. His spirit had brightened when she took the drawing from him. He thought she was going to present it to the class with praise.

She bent over to whisper in his ear as she let the artwork sail back down onto his desk. "Maybe a little less clowning around and a little more effort would help."

He nodded in bewildered defeat.

He waited until she was a safe distance away from him, then looked down at his drawing again and smiled. Despite Mrs. Mullin's dissatisfaction, he had made an effort and was pleased with his creation. He thought the horse was pretty good, and he was proud of it.

Thomas was confused. His first month as a first-grader was

not going as his mother had promised.

You're gonna have so much fun, honey. You're so cute and sweet and everyone will adore you.

He couldn't figure out what he had done, but it was quite clear to him that Mrs. Mullins just did not care for cute, sweet boys, even though most other people did.

He felt something sharp poke him in the arm and looked over to see Sally Sims smiling at him, pencil in hand. Long, red, comically uneven pigtails framed her freckled face.

"I like it," she whispered.

He smiled and looked down at the brown horse.

"Wanna play after school?" she offered with a newly acquired lisp.

He nodded and smiled even wider as he noticed the gap where one of her front teeth was now missing. He wanted very much to play with Sally after 'th-chool.'

"You be the daddy, okay?" Sally handed him two hairless baby dolls, wrapped tightly in pink blankets. "It's twins. Twin girls, Mary and Tina."

Thomas took a bundle in each arm and shook them gently like she had taught him as he walked around the playroom.

"Wahh! Wahh! The babies are crying, Thomas Paul. I'll warm their bottles while you change their diapers."

He smiled as he pretended to change their diapers, remembering to use the powder as Sally reminded him—they must prevent chafing on the babies' bottoms.

"You feed Mary and I'll feed Tina, okay dear?" She handed him one of the dolls, which just last week had been a baby boy named Joey.

"Yes, dear," he answered.

"Make your voice deep, like a real daddy," she ordered.

"Yes, dear!" he grunted.

The doorbell rang in the distance.

"Sally! Thomas' brother is here to walk him home. Please come down," Sally's mother called up to them.

They came down the stairs, still holding the dolls in their arms.

"You come back anytime now, Thomas, and please tell your mother hello," Sally's mother said.

"Thank you. I will."

Sally took the doll from Thomas and hugged him. "See you at school on Monday."

He smiled and waved as he followed his brother down the driveway.

"Hey Thomas, go long!" Peter instructed, ready to toss the football he was carrying.

Thomas ran ahead a few feet and raised his little arms into the air. The ball sailed over him and as he reached to try and catch it, he tripped over his shoelace and fell to the ground. The ball bounced into the grass as he rolled over, sat up, and dusted the gravel off his stinging palms.

"Aw geez, are you okay?" Peter asked as he picked up the ball.

"Yeah, I think so." Thomas kept on walking, glad they only lived around the corner.

"Let's try again."

"Nah. I don't wanna."

"Come on, I'll toss you an easy one. Promise." He placed his fingers in between the white laces and perfected his grip.

Thomas sighed. They were almost home.

"Okay. But don't throw it hard, you're bigger than me." He took a few tentative steps and lifted his arms once more. The ball left his brother's hand and came directly at him. Again, he ran ahead to catch it and was now almost on his front lawn. From the corner of his eye, he could see his father's car pull into the driveway. A second later, he felt the sharp sting of the ball land in his small hands but despite his clumsy attempt at hot potato with the rough pigskin, it slipped through his fingers onto the ground.

"Fumble! Fumble!" his brother yelled as he ran to snatch up the ball.

The car door slammed and his father emerged from the paneled station wagon, tie loosened around his neck and sleeves rolled up.

He said nodding, "Boys. Nice throw, son. Get my suitcase from the trunk and take it to your mother, please." Peter obeyed immediately. Their father, a military man, was stern and strict and had taught his children from a very young age the meaning of the word *respect*. He would never have to ask them more than once to do anything.

"You almost had it there, Thomas Paul." He smiled down at his younger son. "Have you been a good boy for your mom this week?"

Thomas nodded, eager to please.

His father worked out of town, Monday to Friday, every single week of every single month, selling medicine to doctors, so they can help people get better. This was how it was explained to him just last year when he asked why daddy was gone so much. As time went on, Thomas began to notice that things were a lot better in the house when his dad was home. The fridge was fuller, meals were eaten on time, the laundry was done, his siblings got along better and most of all, his mother was happier.

*   *   *

He swirled the toothbrush around in his mouth, gave each molar a half-hearted scrub, spat and rinsed. He dropped the brush into the cup then carefully cleaned the sink as his mother had asked him to do. He padded down the hallway in his pajamas, on his way downstairs to wish his mother goodnight. He paused at the top of the stairs, hearing his mother and father in conversation.

"I don't like him playing with those fucking dolls," his father complained.

"When was he playing with dolls?"

"Today, with that Sims girl. Peter picked him up and he had a doll in his hand. No wonder he can't catch a goddamn football."

"Oh, for Christ's sake, Johnny, he's just a little boy," his mother reassured.

"Exactly." His tone was hushed but harsh at the same time. "He's a boy, and boys shouldn't play with dolls."

"Well, maybe if you were home more …."

He decided to make his way down into the living room with heavy, hurried steps, in hopes of interrupting his father's angry, impatient reply.

The small room was cloudy with cigarette smoke. A highball glass sat sweating on the coffee table, a handful of shiny ice cubes melting inside. "Are you ready for bed, sugar?" His mother smiled and held her arms out to him. He climbed into her lap and hugged her, inhaling the soft, comforting scent of her perfume, a faint smell of beer on her lips. He took a deep breath and rested his head on her shoulder.

She smoothed his hair with her hands and rubbed his back. "I love you, Thomas Paul."

"I love you, Mommy." He climbed off her lap and turned to face his father. "Goodnight-night, Daddy."

His father ruffled his hair and smiled. "Goodnight, son. Don't forget to say your prayers."

He climbed under the covers, confused, as he replayed their words in his head. Why was it bad that he played with dolls? He didn't understand, but he vowed that if it would make his father happy, he would try not to do it anymore. He rolled over and yawned—drifting off to sleep.

He awoke in the middle of the night and could hear his brother's and sisters' muffled sleeping sounds in the room. He sat up and looked around, unsure of what time it was. He moved slowly, careful not to make a sound while he tiptoed over to his brother's bed. He stood next to him, his breath silent, and lifted the sheet to peak at his brother's nearly naked body. The new nightlight gave off just enough of a glow for him to examine Peter's shape. He gazed at the bulge between his brother's legs.

The outline of his penis was clearly visible through his underwear. He had seen it many times when they had bathed together, but now it looked much larger and seemed stiff. Piqued with childish curiosity, he could not help himself and gave it a light poke, causing his brother to shift and roll over. Thomas Paul's heart jumped at his brother's movement and he darted back to his own bed and closed his eyes, feeling 'funny' about what he had just done.

Three nights later, he sat up in the darkness once again. The snoring and shifting sounds of his sleeping siblings were familiar and comforting. As he listened, he heard something else, faint girlish laughter. His small feet touched the cool, wood floor and he stood up, careful not to let his mattress creak. He tiptoed into the hallway, holding his breath with each step.

As he walked down the stairs, a new mixture of scents filled his nostrils. Cigarette smoke, men's cologne that he had never smelled on his father, and something else permeated the air in the small living room. He let his eyes adjust to the dimness and focused on the sofa. There was a large lump, hidden under the colorful afghan knitted by his grandmother. Peeking out from beneath the blanket was a smooth, naked, creamy-white leg.

"Oh, yeah," his mother whispered in a tone he had never heard before. The lump shifted back and forth.

"Mommy? What are you doing?" he asked.

The lump stopped moving. Silence. Then her voice, tense and firm. "Mommy fell asleep on the couch tonight, honey. I was dreaming. You go on back to bed now."

He climbed back into his bed and moments later, heard the door to the house open and close. He closed his eyes and wondered why his mother slept on the couch so often when his daddy was on the road. He hoped she wasn't scared.

Chapter 3

"Goddamnit, Carol! What are you doing? What have you done?!" his father shouted at the top of his lungs.

"I'm sorry, John. Oh, please, Johnny. I'm sorry. I'm so sorry," his mother pleaded.

"Jesus H-fucking Christ! You pissed yourself! You pissed all over the brand new couch that you made me buy!"

Thomas Paul and his siblings stayed silent in their bedroom. Thomas was confused. Mommy peed her pants? Poor Mommy. Why was Daddy so mad at her? Maybe it was the operation last year, when they took part of her insides out. Mommy had explained that since she wasn't having any more kids, her 'uterus' needed to come out but that she would be fine. But she wasn't fine. Sometimes she was sad and stared off into space, like she was in a dream, only she was awake with her eyes open. For a long time, Thomas was worried that the doctor had taken out Mommy's happiness along with her 'uterus'.

"Please help me, Johnny. I don't know what's wrong with me." Her voice was desperate. *Thomas wanted to run downstairs to her.*

His father spoke into the phone for a moment, then slammed the receiver back into its cradle.

His grandparents showed up within minutes, loaded her into the car, and then she was gone for a while. The house was quiet in her absence and Cecile, the nanny who came to take care of them until mommy came back, helped make things better. When his daddy came home on the weekends, he acted the same as always. The kids knew to stay out of his way. Finally, after being gone for two weeks, his mother came home. She was happy and things were good again. No one talked about her accident on the couch — the stain had been removed by a man name Carl, the carpet cleaner.

*   *   *

Thomas strutted out to the edge of the diving board, bounced once and dove with confidence and ease into the cool, crisp water. He felt his fingers touch the rough concrete bottom of the pool and he pushed himself up, smiling as he kicked his feet and fluttered to the surface. He popped his head out of the water, refilled his lungs, and squinted. His ears followed the sound of his mother's clapping. She was reclined in a beach chair, up on the concrete deck that bordered the pool and the lake.

"Way to go, Thomas Paul!" She smiled at him, lounging in a bright cover up. She didn't wear her bikini anymore. She had always been so petite, even after four kids, but now, after putting on some weight in the last year, she had retired her two-piece suit. Still, she was bronzed from the sun, her blond hair bright after hours spent at the pool or at Rough River on the weekends, when his father was home.

It was her turn. She arose from her chair, tucked her hair into a bathing cap, dropped her cover-up, and sauntered over to the diving tower facing the lake. She climbed up the ladder, walked to the edge of the tallest, third platform and jumped, laughing as she held her nose on the way down into the cool water. Thomas and his siblings, bobbing up and down in the pool, clapped for her. She came to the surface, a wide smile on her face, and swam the length of the lake until she reached the wooden floating dock at the other end. The children watched her with pride. She was an accomplished swimmer and covered the distance in no time. It relieved Thomas to see her healthy and happy. He had worried that she would never be herself again after the incident with the couch and her subsequent trip to the special hospital.

For now, summer was heaven. The pool was endless joy, fun, and freedom. He never wanted it to end and yet he was excited for school to start again.

*   *   *

"Line up!" the P.E. teacher bellowed into a bullhorn. Thomas Paul's stomach tightened. Mrs. Stucker was a buxom brunette, tall and fit, her athletic body tanned and toned. She kept her long fingernails painted in the same bright red as the Mustang she drove and always wore a matching sun visor to complete her look. She could run, jump, throw, and sweat with the students all day long, but her makeup never seemed to run or smear. A whistle around her neck bounced between her breasts with every step.

Thomas Paul, like all the other kids, was in awe of her and

wanted so much for Mrs. Stucker to like him. Unfortunately, she took pleasure in berating the kids, male or female, who didn't excel at sports. It was obvious that she had no patience for Thomas and the few other kids who lacked any athletic talent.

"It's competition day, and this counts toward your grade," she continued. Boys and girls pushed and shoved each other, some to get in the front of the line to demonstrate their athletic abilities—others, mortified at what was sure to be an exercise in humiliation, fell to the back. Thomas stood in the back of the line behind Mavis Burns, another hapless misfit in his class who would sit with him at lunchtime.

"Oh, joy," Mavis whispered.

"Maybe the bell will ring before we get our turn," Thomas Paul answered. It was more of a prayer than a comment.

"First, the softball throw," the teacher explained, "everyone will put on the baseball glove and have to catch and throw the ball." She continued talking, but Thomas Paul's mind had drifted off.

"Come on, son, try harder," his father said as he tossed him the ball again, only to see it tumble out of the glove and fall to the ground.

"Why did you have to be left-handed?" his father sighed.

I am trying, Thomas Paul thought to himself while fidgeting with Peter's right-handed glove that he was forced to wear because nobody would take the time to buy him a left-handed one. If his father only knew how hard he was really trying.

"Follow through, okay? Put your shoulder into it. Ready?"

Thomas took a deep breath and mustered all his strength. He closed his eyes and threw the ball as far as he could. Seconds later, he heard it thud onto the ground, and he opened his eyes.

His father shook his head at the sight of the ball, laying only a few yards in front of him.

Thomas looked down at his feet, happy that his father was spending time with him but wishing they could do something else.

"Okay Thomas, one last time. Here we go!" He clapped his hands together a few times, offered an impatient smile, and waited.

Inhale. Eyes closed. Toss. Thud. Eyes peeking open, praying that the ball was farther across the yard. Exhale.

"Goddamnit, Thomas Paul, can't you do anything right? You just don't give a shit, that's why you can't throw a fucking ball!" Moments later the door to the house slammed shut.

*   *   *

The sound of clapping interrupted his reverie. Andrew Jones, the most athletic boy in class, maybe even in the whole school, was at the front of the line. He warmed up his arm by making wide, slow circles in each direction.

"Go, Andrew!"

"Do it, man!" his classmates encouraged him.

Mrs. Stucker smiled as she tossed Andrew the ball and he caught it in his bare hand. He moved away from the line of kids to give himself room and got into the proper pitching position—he was a real baseball player. He wound up and threw the ball underhanded. It sailed through the air and when it finally hit the ground, even without Mrs. Stucker's measuring tape, it was evident that Andrew's ball would be the farthest thrown by anyone that day.

"Stanton! Your turn."

Thomas Paul's heart sank. In all the excitement of gathering around and jostling to watch and congratulate Andrew, a new line had formed, and Thomas found himself standing in the front. Nobody wanted to throw the ball after Andrew, least of all Thomas.

"We don't have a left-handed glove, so you'll just have to use a right-handed one," Mrs. Stucker said.

He may not have been athletic, but Thomas and everyone else knew it was crazy for a left-handed person to be using a right-handed glove. All eyes were now on him, and he felt the color rise in his cheeks.

"Here...catch." She lobbed the ball towards him, and he held out his hand. The ball rolled out of the glove and onto the dirt.

His peers snickered, and he felt a bead of sweat roll down his back. *Please let the bell ring. Please let the bell ring.*

"Just pick it up and throw it," she said, ready with the tape measure and clipboard in her hand.

Thomas gripped the ball in his sweaty hand. He envisioned it sailing high into the air and flying farther than anyone else's ball. He imagined Mrs. Stucker's reaction: her wide eyes, her jaw dropped open, beaming at him as she announced how far his ball had gone. If only she knew just how much he wanted to please her.

Everyone was still, and a collective inhale could be heard as the ball left his fingers.

It landed with an audible thud, and Mrs. Stucker smiled as she walked out to measure the distance.

She started laughing into the bullhorn.

"Stanton only threw the ball forty feet! He can't even throw it as far as a girl."

The whole class, except for Mavis, erupted into howling laughter.

"Let's make up a new name for Stanton. How about Sissy Stanton? That's what we'll call him from now on...Sissy Stanton!"

His humiliation was complete. The backwards glove, his pitiful throw, the laughter, and now the nickname—he wanted the ground to open up and swallow him whole.

Finally, the bell rang. As the laughter died down, Mavis put her hand on his shoulder and squeezed it.

"Just ignore them."

But that was easier said than done. He would walk the hallways with many of these kids for the rest of his youth, and they wouldn't forget. He would be Sissy Stanton for what seemed like forever.

As they made their way back into the school, Andrew Jones sidled up to him and put his hand on Thomas' shoulder.

"Don't worry about it, Thomas. It's only a stupid ball throw."

Thomas looked at him and could see the sincerity in his face. They exchanged mutual half smiles before Andrew ran on to join his friends.

Despite this unexpected show of kindness, Thomas Paul felt something change inside him. Years later, he would look back and realize that his spirit was broken that day. It would stay that way for a long time.

"Are you okay?" Sally asked him as they walked home after school. If they timed it right, Thomas would often take a different route home and wait for the bus to drop Sally off.

Thomas shrugged. "Does it really matter if I can't throw a ball?" he asked, after recounting the story of his miserable day.

"No, it doesn't." She grabbed his hand and held it for a moment as they walked, waiting to see what he would do.

"It sure matters to my dad. It matters to Stucker. It matters to everyone else in the class." Angry, he squeezed her hand but did not let go.

"It doesn't matter to me." Sally stopped walking and pulled his hand so he would stop, too.

Thomas Paul looked at her, and despite his preoccupation with the awful school day, he could sense something different in her gaze. She was his best friend, his only friend, but she was looking at him in the same way she had first stared at him back in the first grade. He felt himself blush and dropped her hand. He was surprised, flattered, and confused all at the same time.

He walked into the house, his spirits lifted.

"Hi, honey, how was school?" his mother asked, deflating his mood as quickly as Sally had brightened it.

"Horrible." Thomas Paul slumped into a kitchen chair. He recounted his day and his humiliation, from the backwards glove all the way to the demeaning nickname that pierced his heart.

His mother was angry and vowed to do something about it. No teacher was going to treat her son that way. Thomas Paul was comforted by her protection—finally, someone would stand up for him. But his comfort was short-lived. There was no call to the school, not even a note. What followed instead were comments and advice that only helped fuel his insecurity.

"You need to toughen up. If only you liked sports Thomas Paul. If you want to fit in, you're going to have to start liking sports." His mother knew that her son didn't fit in. She truly wanted him to have friends and not be picked on. His parents

were   like   everyone   else;   they   wanted   him   to
be something and someone that he wasn't.

Chapter 4

Thomas walked home alone, his stomach in knots. School was torture. He was well-liked by some of his teachers, but that didn't make up for the disdain he felt from his peers. He just couldn't seem to fit in anywhere. It was a cruel irony to learn that being good-looking but having no athletic ability was just as much a curse as being fat, homely, and pimply faced.

The lack of friendship, attention, or simple acknowledgement only made Thomas Paul crave it more. He would try to catch some of the boys' eyes, even offer a light smile. *Hey! See me! Talk to me! Like me! Accept me!*

He floundered around in the sea of adolescence—lonely, scared, and clueless as to the ways of friendship. A misfit. The more he lacked the natural camaraderie between boys, the more he sought it out. His awkwardness only fueled his schoolmates' intolerance of him. They saw his kindness and shyness as feminine, and Thomas Paul perceived them recoiling from him, even snickering as he walked past them.

He retreated into himself and as his teachers droned on, he zoned out and passed his school days fantasizing about being accepted and popular. He daydreamed about the popular girls that he had crushes on. And lately, he often thought about P.E. class and showering with other boys—all of them naked. A part of him felt a twinge of hesitation at thinking such things. He knew from church that boys were not supposed to be together that way. But these were his private thoughts and he could think what he wanted. Nobody would know.

It was Friday, and unlike, for most other kids in the world, it was becoming his least favorite day. At school, he could stay out of the way. Invisible. As unwelcome as it was, often times it was an escape. Home, on the other hand, was slowly becoming his least favorite place to be in the whole world. There was nowhere to hide at home.

Things were changing, and he didn't know why. His mother was losing her grip on her mind, and with that went his father's patience and sense of reasoning.

The ache in his stomach grew sharper as he approached the house.

Thomas held his breath as he opened the door, trying his best not to make any noise. His sister, Anne Marie, was already home, a panicked look on her face as she surveyed the kitchen. Their older brother was nowhere to be found, undoubtedly seeking refuge with his friends, as usual. Their little sister was also nowhere to be found, which often seemed to be the norm as well, leaving Thomas and Anne Marie to handle things.

"Thomas Paul, I told you to clean this up before we left for school so it would be done before Daddy got home." Her whisper was filled with desperate worry. "Quick, get the scrubber and clean the jelly off the counter top."

Thomas rummaged around the kitchen in a hurried panic and finally found the scrubber but in his haste slammed, the cabinet door shut. The sound echoed through the small house. He and Anne Marie froze.

"How many times do I have to tell you fucking kids to be quiet when I am sleeping!" his mother screeched in a fragile, shaky voice. "I do for you and do for you and all I ask in return is for you to be quiet when I'm sleeping!"

Anne Marie stared at him with accusing eyes. *Now look what you did!*

"I'm sorry," Thomas said.

"I told you to be quiet!" his sister hissed.

"I said shut your fucking mouths, you ungrateful brats! If I have to get up from here to shut you up, you'll both be sorry!" his mother screamed on. "Oh, what am I gonna do? What am I gonna do? Your daddy's on his way home and I'm sick and can't get any sleep."

She was yelling at the top of her lungs now—at the kids, at the heavens, and at nobody in particular. "You kids better get this fucking house cleaned up so your daddy doesn't beat you when he gets here. You know I can't handle it when he gets mad!"

Tears welled in Thomas Paul's eyes, and he forced a heavy lump back down his throat, forbidding it from forming into a sob and escaping from his mouth. There was no use crying right now. It would only make things worse, and there was nobody to comfort him anyway, not anymore, not for a long time now. He scrubbed the kitchen counter as hard as he could and scurried around the house in silence, trying to get it clean.

His stomach churned as he watched the clock. It was only a matter of time until his father came home, and Thomas had learned that it really didn't matter how hard he tried to make things right, sooner or later, things would be wrong. They always were.

"Thomas Paul! Get your ass up these fucking steps right now!"

With his eyes wide and his pulse racing, Thomas ran up the stairs and stood in front of his father.

"Did you do this?" He pointed to a pile of clothes stuffed into Thomas Paul's closet.

"Yes, Daddy, but..." It didn't matter that there had been no laundry soap left and that Thomas had merely put the dirty clothes out of sight until somebody made it to the store.

"You'd better hold off on those 'buts' Thomas Paul, or I'll whip you harder for saying 'em. Either you did it or you didn't do it. Which is it?"

Thomas lowered his head. "Yes."

"Yes what?"

"Yes sir, I did it."

His father pulled off his shoe. "Bend over this stool, goddamnit."

Thomas hesitated for a second.

"Right now, before I really lose my temper!"

"How-many-fucking-times-do-I-have-to-tell-you-kids-not-to-do-a-shitass-half-assed-job-at-things!" Each word was punctuated by a blow to Thomas Paul's backside.

"Now," his father caught his breath as he ceased the beating and pointed to the door, shoe still in hand, "go to your room, clean that mess up, and get ready for church." Thomas Paul sobbed in uncontrollable heaves, bubbles blowing out of his nose, and pushed himself up from the stool.

"Y-y-y-es sir."

His father turned and stormed into Anne Marie's bedroom.

"Now it's your turn, Anne Marie. Who do you think you are, young lady?" He held up her purse, filled with makeup and stared at her.

"I'm sorry, Daddy. I know I'm not supposed to but..." She shook as she spoke, having seen what he'd done to her brother and seeing the rage in his eyes now, she bolted down the steps.

"You can run if you want, but when I get my hands on you, I will beat you 'til you can't walk, little girl." There was an almost eerie calm in his voice now, like he wasn't himself and was almost pleased that she had run.

Thomas Paul stood in the bathroom and listened to his father barreling down the stairs after his sister. He was in awe that she had run from him. What was she thinking? It would surely be worse for her now it always was.

"Daddy, please! No, Daddy!"

Thomas looked at his reflection in the mirror: eyes red, snot running, cheeks wet with tears. He bent down and splashed cold water on his face, over and over again. He turned off the faucet and could still hear his father yelling over the soft thumping—a broomstick that he had broken on her thighs. His sister's pleas for mercy subsided.

"Now, march upstairs and throw every bit of that shit away. I better never catch you with it again," he ordered.

Thomas opened the medicine cabinet. He studied the rows of pill bottles on the shelves—his mother's mood elevators, several pills whose names he couldn't pronounce which didn't seem to be helping her. He couldn't remember the last time his mother had been in a good mood. The more he thought about it, the more he realized she wasn't really happy or sad. She wasn't really anything. She was just there—but not there. She slept most of the time, which suited him and his siblings just fine.

Anne Marie banged on the bathroom door, and Thomas let her in. She avoided his eyes. No matter how often it happened, to any of them, it was always a shameful experience.

His father appeared at the bathroom door, and they froze. "You know I love you kids, but you are going to learn to do what I tell you, or else." He didn't wait for a response before walking back down the steps. Thomas swallowed and exhaled.

Thomas Paul winced as he squirmed on the cold, hard, wooden church pew, his bottom still aching from the beating. *Please God, let tomorrow come quickly so Daddy can go back to work.*

After mass, his father paraded his well-behaved brood out of church, shook hands and exchanged pleasantries with several fellow parishioners and friends, and piled his family back into the car.

"Who wants to go to the bakery?" Thomas Paul's father asked, a smile upon his face.

"We do! Yes, please!" the kids answered in unison.

They headed to the bakery with the windows rolled down. It was a beautiful day, the sky clear and bright and the cool breeze blowing in their faces as they rode along. Thomas Paul's mouth watered, thinking about the treats that awaited them at the bakeshop.

His father's mood had lifted, a stark contrast to what it had been before church. After the beating, his sister had dared to keep their father waiting in the driveway his face red with fury as he honked the horn and pounded on the steering wheel.

Inevitably, he would go back inside the house after her and march her out to the car, the possibility of being late for mass the only thing saving her from getting another whipping.

They pulled into the parking lot, and Thomas could smell warm, sweet bakery aromas wafting through the open car windows. The kids jumped out of the car and followed their father into the store.

The clerk smiled. "Good morning, John."

"Morning, Ramona. Fine day out there, isn't it?"

"It sure is."

"Hello, Miss Ramona," the Stanton kids said as they crowded around the glass display cases.

"Hi, kids. What'll it be today?"

"Give us the usual, please. And make sure this young man gets the biggest piece." Thomas Paul's father stood behind him and placed his hands on his younger son's shoulders.

Ramona winked at Thomas. "You got it, blue eyes." She handed him an extra-large slice of warm butterkuchen and Thomas grinned, anxious to taste it.

"Thank you." He smiled at the clerk and then up at his father. "Thanks, Daddy."

Like always, Ramona handed their father a small box containing a slice to take home to their mother.

"Thank you, dear." He handed her some cash.

"You tell lovely Miss Carol hello," Ramona said as she handed their father his change. "Y'all have a great day."

As they sat around the table together enjoying their gooey, sweet confection with cool glasses of milk and breathing in the rich smell of their father's steaming cup of coffee, Thomas noticed that his bottom didn't hurt so much anymore. He wished his father didn't always have to leave every week. 5

Chapter 5

Thomas sat on the bottom front step and stared down at the concrete patio. A stream of ants climbed out, one by one, from a crack in the pavement. They marched single file over to the grass and then back to the entrance in the cement, each one carrying some sort of earthly item in its jaws.

He marveled at their strength and determination, wondering if they spoke to each other in passing while they worked. He peered at them, hypnotized by their routine. They all looked identical, and he wondered if they looked the same to each other. Was one ant prettier than the others? Was one uglier? Were some shy? Were some mean? Did some get picked on? Was there an ant bully? Did they ever work or travel alone? He couldn't recall ever having seen one lone ant. They seemed to work so well together. Not like real people. Not like the kids at school, anyway.

Thomas thought of the morning at school again. A lump formed in his throat. All he had done was *look* at a boy. Simply look him in the eye as they stood in the smoking area outside of school. The older boy stepped away from his friends, walked up to Thomas and glared at him with contempt. Then, after what seemed like several moments, he snorted up as much mucus and saliva as he had available in his mouth and sinus cavities and spat it into Thomas Paul's face.

"Quit looking at me, you fucking faggot," he sneered as the foul spew dripped down from Thomas Paul's eyes to his chin.

Shocked and confused, Thomas froze, terrified of what the boy would do next, but he flicked his cigarette at Thomas Paul's feet and laughed as he and his friends walked off. *Welcome to the seventh grade.*

Thomas stood alone in the bathroom, trembling, and rinsed off his face, too mortified to even cry. The spit hurt more and was more humiliating than if he had been punched in the nose. He stared at his reflection and wondered again just what it was that made some people hate him so. *Apparently, there is a right way and a wrong way to look at someone.*

Thomas Paul's reverie was halted when a shadow loomed over the insect trail and a red drop splashed down on one of the ants, paralyzing it for a moment. Thomas' eyes widened as the ant's feelers twitched with fury from the unexpected moisture.

He looked up to find Sally, smiling as she tilted her melting Popsicle over the squirming bugs.

"Got him. Ha! Whatcha doing?" She slurped the icy treat in her hand, her lips bright red from the sweet cherry stain.

"Nothing. Where'd you get that?"

"From Tinesy."

"Who's Tinesy?" Thomas asked.

"You know, Tinesy. From up the street."

"Oh, yeah. What were you doing there?" Thomas asked.

"Just hanging out."

"Why do you call her Tinesy anyway?"

"Cause she's little. Teensy Tinesy. Everyone calls her that. Do you want to meet her?"

Thomas shrugged. "Okay." He looked down. The ants had long since resumed their daily duties, and he was careful to step over them as he followed Sally.

They approached the house, Thomas trailing a few feet behind Sally. There were several kids of all different ages running around while someone hung wet laundry on a clothesline. Sally grabbed Thomas' hand and pulled him over to the line.

Tinesy was little indeed. She stood on a stool to reach the clotheslines with the laundry basket on a table next to her to make all the bending and reaching easier. She was pretty and still shapely after having three kids.

She spotted them as they approached. "Hey there. You're back. Did you forget something, honey?" She smiled and climbed off her stool.

"Nope. Just wanted you to meet my friend."

"This is Tommy."

"Hello, Tommy." Tinesy looked up at him. "You're the younger Stanton boy, aren't you?"

"Yes ma'am. Hello." Thomas smiled.

Tinesy turned to Sally and winked. "You didn't tell me your boyfriend was such a looker."

Sally and Thomas both laughed.

"He's not my boyfriend. We're just best friends."

"Well, too bad for you, Sally. I wouldn't leave this handsome boy alone if I were you!"

She turned to Thomas and touched his arm. "Tommy, you're welcome here any time."

"Thank you," he answered.

"You need some help with the laundry?" Sally offered.

"That would be great, y'all."

Thomas and Sally hung the sheets and towels while Tinesy pinned the smaller items on the line. Kids ran in and out of the damp laundry, screaming and laughing.

"Get out of the clothes! I mean it, y'all better listen to me!" Tinesy hollered and shooed them away.

"Where did all these kids come from?" Sally asked as she stacked the empty baskets inside one another. Thomas took them from Sally and carried them to the house.

Tinesy rolled her eyes. "Well, six of them are Sadie's kids."

"Sadie?" Sally said.

"You know, Sadie, the Jesus freak. Lives around the corner." Tinesy beckoned them to follow her inside. "Sit, sit." She gestured for them to sit at the kitchen table, then stood on her tiptoes, reached into the cabinet for three glasses, and poured them each a glass of icy lemonade. "You mean you've never heard of Sadie?"

Thomas and Sally shook their heads in unison.

"Nice enough lady, if you keep your distance. Get too close to her though, and you're bound to feel her judgmental eyes boring into you," she laughed and looked out the window to watch the kids in the backyard.

"Really?" Sally was intrigued.

Tinesy joined them at the table. "Let me tell you, some of us ladies got together for tea once, and she was invited. Wasn't long before she started spouting off about the Lord and salvation and eternal damnation and such, it was crazy. The tea wasn't even lukewarm, and the place cleared out. Sadie hasn't been invited to tea since." She sipped her lemonade and went back over to the window.

"Funny though, for such a religious nut, her kids are wild."

She pushed open the door. "All my kids, inside to wash up for dinner! All you other kids go on home, please!"

Thomas and Sally finished their drinks and placed the empty glasses in the sink.

"Thanks for the lemonade, Tinesy. We're gonna go now," Sally said.

"Oh, thank you, kids, for the help with the laundry. Y'all come back anytime."

"She's cool, huh?" Sally asked as they walked back to Thomas's house.

"Yeah. And you're right, she *is* tinesy." Thomas laughed.

As they neared the house, they spotted a strange car in the driveway and another pulling up. An orange Chevy Chevelle came to a stop alongside the curb, and four young girls exited the car. They were Anne Marie's girlfriends. Two carried large pizza boxes and another held a paper grocery bag filled to the brim. Thomas wasn't familiar with two of the girls who climbed out of the car, whispering and giggling. They smiled at him as they walked past. Thomas did not look twelve, and had any stranger spotted them all together on the street, it would have been easy to believe that they were just a group of sixteen- year-olds hanging out together. The driver, May Hall, emerged last.

"Hi, Tommy." She smiled at him as she walked by. Her long blonde hair hung down her back and swayed as she walked. Her perfume lingered in the air for a moment after she passed.

"Is your sister having a party?"

"I guess so."

"Your mom doesn't care?"

"Nuh-uh. She likes it when Anne Marie has friends over."

"Well, they sure noticed you." Sally looked away, her voice tinged with jealousy.

Thomas shrugged off her comment, unsure of what to say. He was aware that Sally had been acting different lately and wondered if it was because she wanted to be his girlfriend. "I gotta go." Sally didn't wait for a goodbye before turning away from him. With quick steps, she crossed the street and disappeared up the sidewalk.

Thomas watched her leave but wasn't thinking about what had just transpired between them; he was distracted.

He couldn't stop thinking about Sadie, the Jesus freak. There was something missing in his life that he simply wasn't getting at home or at school. He started to wonder if maybe God was the answer, and even though nobody else seemed to care for Sadie, he could relate to that. *Salvation* didn't sound so bad to him at all.

He walked back into the house and could hear music playing. His mother sat in her usual spot at the kitchen table, drinking beer and smoking.

"Hi, honey," she said, sipping from a sweaty Coors can.

"Hi, Mom," Thomas said. He kissed her on the cheek then flopped down in the chair next to her. He could hear laughter from the basement. Not just his sister and her friends but male laughter, too. This was why his mother let Anne Marie have parties during the week. Had his father been home, there would have been no such co-ed festivities taking place and no beer drinking.

His sister came upstairs to use the bathroom. When she was finished, she came into the kitchen.

"Hey, wanna come down?"

"Really?" Thomas said.

She laughed. "Some of the girls were asking where my hunky brother was."

His mother smiled. "Go on, honey," she said with a subtle slur, almost halfway into the case of beer in the fridge. She shooed him along, unaware of the make-out party that was going on in her basement. Or, maybe it was the opposite. Maybe she knew exactly what was going on down there.

Thomas followed Anne Marie down the stairs. He scanned the room with timid eyes. There were two boys he recognized, two he'd never seen before who must have been older, and the girls from outside. They greeted him warmly and before long they all sat on the floor in a circle, a green glass bottle in the center of their group. Laughter, clapping, and squeals followed as the bottle spun and partners were chosen for awkward, impromptu kisses.

Soon, it was May's turn to spin. Sitting across from Thomas, she smiled at him as she gave the bottle a gentle twist, just enough so that it ended up pointing directly at him.

Thomas blushed in the dim light as pretty, sixteen-year-old May crawled over to him and placed her mouth on his. The blood rushed through his body as their lips touched, and he felt his palms moisten. Aware that he was being watched.

Thomas closed his eyes and tried to act like this wasn't his first real kiss. May opened her mouth slightly, and he followed her lead. She tasted like bubblegum. Soon, the others were hooting and hollering at the length of the kiss, and although he had no desire to do so, Thomas pulled away and joined in the laughter.

For the rest of the game, they glanced at one another with flirtatious eyes, and Thomas sensed that the other girls made sure not to spin the bottle so that it would land in front of him again. At the end of the night, Anne Marie cornered him in the small basement.

"May really likes you. You should call her sometime," she whispered.

"Really? But she's...your friend. Are you sure?" Thomas tried to act cool, like he wasn't stunned by what his sister was telling him and not the twelve-year-old kid that he actually was. He tried to act as old as he looked.

"Of course. I'm going to tell her that I will give you her number, okay?" she continued.

"Okay." He could feel May staring at them, and he mustered up the courage to wave to her as she and the other girls started up the stairs to leave.

He had trouble falling asleep that night, images of May clouding his thoughts. He was elated. Giddy that a girl so much older than he was actually liked him. He would call her tomorrow. But what would he say? They didn't even go to the same school. Thank God, he thought. At least she wouldn't see what a friendless misfit he was. For the moment, Sadie and salvation were out of his mind.

"What do you mean 'you're going together'?" Sally asked as she got up and turned down the television.

"Just like I said, we're boyfriend and girlfriend." Thomas said.

"But she's sixteen! You're twelve. Does she know you're *twelve?*" They sat on the couch at Sally's house, watching a now-silent episode of *Happy Days.*

"I look older." Thomas protested. "She doesn't care."

Sally started pacing the room.

"And your parents don't care? *Your* mom doesn't care that you are dating someone that much older than you?"

"No. They drive me to her place to hang out sometimes," Thomas said, matter-of-factly. They were thrilled that he was showing an interest in girls, and not just any girl but a beautiful girl whom they knew and liked. Finally, he had made them proud—but only after several reminders from his mother about how to treat girls. *You have to respect girls. You NEVER ever hit a girl. Girls are fragile, delicate. If I ever hear of you mistreating a girl, I don't care how old you are, Thomas Paul, I will come after you.* The warnings were always followed by stories of how she was mistreated by men, mostly his father. *Your daddy is so mean. I couldn't stand it if you turned out like him.* He would learn years later that not only did his mother's admonitions instill in him a strong sense of respect for girls but fear of them, as well.

Sally stopped pacing and stared at him. Out of arguments, she flopped back down on the couch.

"Have you kissed her?"

"Yeah. We kissed that night when my sister had the party," he said, his voice filled with pride.

Sally frowned.

"I didn't think you'd react like this," Thomas lied.

"Neither did I," she mumbled under her breath.

"What do you mean?"

"Nothing. I don't mean anything." She stood up and turned off the TV. "I have homework I need to do. You should go."

Confused and saddened by Sally's coolness towards him, he embarked on a different route home. A few minutes later, he slowed his pace as he approached Sadie's house. She stood in the front yard, watering flowers. She was fair-haired and attractive. She turned around, almost as if she felt she was being watched.

"Hello," she said, smiling. She put down her watering can and wiped her hands on the apron she wore.

"Hi." Thomas waved and returned her smile.

"You live in the neighborhood, don't you? Haven't I seen you over at Tinesy's?"

"Yes, I live just around the corner. I'm Thomas Paul. My friend Sally and I go to Tinesy's a lot."

"Do you babysit, Thomas Paul? I'm always looking for new babysitters," she continued.

"Sure." He found himself eager to possibly spend more time with her, even if it meant looking after her six kids for an afternoon or evening.

"Why don't you come inside for a bit?" She held out her arm to usher him inside.

The interior of the house was a direct contradiction to Sadie's outward appearance. It was complete chaos inside the house. Toys, clothes, and dirty dishes were strewn everywhere. The kitchen sink was filled with more unwashed dishes, and food sat all over the counters and the table. Mismatched shoes of all different sizes littered the floor, and books and papers were stacked on chairs and any flat surface around the house.

It was familiar to him. It reminded Thomas of the condition of his own home when his father was out of town. He noticed several portraits and pictures of Jesus hanging on the walls and large, ornate crosses hanging over the front and back doorways. His eyes lingered on them for a moment.

As if sensing his thoughts, she questioned him. "Have you been saved, Thomas Paul?"

He swallowed and nodded his head. "Yes, ma'am."

"So you're a Christian? Your family is Christian?"

"Yes. Catholic, ma'am." Wasn't that the same thing?

Sadie shook her head. "Catholics aren't true Christians, Thomas. There is no mention of any pope in the Bible. Do you read the Bible?"

"No, ma'am. It's not allowed. Well, we're only supposed to read the Bible with a priest…." His voice trailed off.

"Well now, you see? How silly is that? You've been taught not to read the Lord's holy word and to simply believe what a bunch of pagans have told you throughout the years. True Christians read the Bible every single day. "

Thomas hung on her every word and made a mental note to look up 'pagan' in the dictionary when he got home.

"Would you like to read the Bible?" She waited. "Would you like to be saved, Thomas Paul?"

"Yes, ma'am." At that moment, he'd never wanted anything more in his entire life. He truly believed that it would offer an escape from some of his torment.

"You can call me Sadie. I'm so glad you stopped by today." She gave him a warm smile and reached out to hug him. Her firm embrace was nurturing and comforting.

"Let's sit." She led him to the couch and cleared enough space for the two of them to sit down. "Tell me about yourself." She crossed her hands in her lap and waited.

So he did. There wasn't much to tell except the basics. Of course, he left out any details that were embarrassing, like his mother's mental issues, his father's fierce temper, and his miserable, friendless existence at school. He also excluded any details that he thought she would disapprove of, like his older girlfriend. In time, though, she would become his best friend and would know almost everything about him. He would spend as much time with her as he could, reading the Bible and talking for hours about Jesus and the fiery damnation of hell — where he would surely go if he remained Catholic.

He felt almost guilty as they read the Bible together and even more so as he snuck away to attend church with her family on Sunday nights, after having sat in the pew next to his father those very same mornings at St. Martin's.

"Why are you so late?" his mother asked him as he walked in the house late one Sunday evening. "You have school in the morning, Thomas Paul."

"I was at Sadie's, and she came home late," he said.

His mother rolled her eyes. "You mean that woman who talks about religion with you? What were you doing over there?"

"I was babysitting the kids while they went to church. The two littlest ones are sick," he lied.

"Hmmm. May called twice, wondering where you were. You should call her back before it's too late."

"Thanks. I will." He grabbed the receiver in the kitchen as he dialed her number and then stretched the cord all the way into the bathroom so he could talk to her in private.

"Hello," she answered.

"Hey."

"Hey!" She was excited to hear his voice. "I called twice. How are you?"

"I'm good. Just watching some of Sadie's kids. What's going on?"

"Nothing. I miss you." He could hear the smile in her voice.

He missed her, too. She was the only thing that could take his mind off Jesus and Sadie's preaching. They talked for a long time, not really saying much of anything, just simply taking comfort in each other's voice.

"Can you come over tomorrow? My parents will be out late. We'll be alone," she whispered.

"Sure. My mom can bring me." The thought of being alone with her titillated him and scared him at the same time. He sensed that she expected and wanted him to do things with her that any other boy her age would do, but he hadn't the foggiest idea what those things were.

"I have to go. I love you," she said.

"I love you, too. Goodnight."

He emerged from the bathroom and replaced the phone in its cradle. His parents sat in the living room, smiling at him as he passed through on his way upstairs to his room.

"Was that May?" his father asked.

"Yeah. Mom, can you take me over to hang out for a bit tomorrow?" he asked.

"Sure, honey," she answered without hesitation.

"I sure do like that May, son," his father proclaimed.

"Me too. Well, goodnight." He retreated to his room and fell asleep to thoughts of May and how she loved it when he ran his fingers through her long blonde locks.

The next night, they sat together in May's living room, making out and listening to records on her parents' stereo.

"They won't be home until 9:30, so we have until then to … do whatever," she giggled.

They lay on the couch, pressing their bodies against one another as they kissed, a small moan escaping from Thomas' throat. In an invisible fog of teenage lust and hormones, they panted as they rocked together and rolled around on the lumpy sofa, taking turns being on top of one another— in hopes that the other would know what to do and where to touch. May seemed pleased with the effect she always had on him. She arched her back, offering herself to him, yearning for him to explore and experiment with her, but he couldn't bring himself to go any further.

She was sixteen and ready to do things her friends were doing but Thomas Paul was twelve, and although he looked her age, he was still very much a boy in a young man's body. Their evenings together were a sexually confusing mixture of hope, desire, and wonder. Thomas felt his pulse quicken as May's hands roamed over his body but he knew he would go home again later, frustrated and with a notable pain in his groin — their passion repeatedly doused by each other's insecurity and inexperience.

One evening, a few weeks later, the phone rang. They hadn't gone this long without talking or seeing each other since the first make-out party in his basement. Thomas Paul hesitantly put the phone to his ear. He knew she wanted to end it. *Things just aren't working out and maybe we should take a break.* He felt   crushed—he loved her. But she is sixteen and he is twelve. Months later, it occurred to him that she dumped him for another boy—a boy with a driver's license.

CHAPTER 6

Thomas Paul closed his eyes and tried to sleep but could not get the image out of his mind. It had been weeks since he had piled in the car with his siblings and his mother, her case of Coors beer chilling in a cooler in the trunk, to watch *The Exorcist* at the drive-in. It was a much anticipated summer ritual for them, to load up the car and see the latest movies together as a family. That night had been no exception. This latest horror film had captivated audiences all over the nation, and they were eager to see what all the fuss was about.

Sadie had warned him—blasphemous, she called it. Thomas Paul prayed for God to erase the visions from his head of a demonized Linda Blair spewing sickening green vomit from her mouth. He feared Sadie may have been right. It wasn't only his thoughts that were terrifying him; something was happening to his mother again. He sensed it that night at the drive-in, watching her, as she stared at the screen with glassy eyes. He wanted her to comfort him and reassure him that it was only a silly movie, just make-believe, but he could see from her face that she was as terrified as he was.

She had not said a word on the drive home. Only three of the chilled beers were left in the Styrofoam cooler, bobbing up and down like buoys in the cold water, but she was steady at the wheel, almost overly focused on the road. In truth, her mind had been playing tricks on her again for weeks, maybe even months, but Thomas and his siblings were oblivious— or in denial. Either way, it didn't matter. If there was some sort of evil seed sprouting in his mother's mind before that night, *The Exorcist* had injected it with a sinister fertilizer and nurtured it into a full-blown poisonous vine with deep roots that wrapped around her thoughts, choking off any sign of reality or reason.

Finally, overcome with fatigue, Thomas felt sleep enveloping him. He was so thankful to be rid of the images, both real and imagined, for at least a few hours.

In the morning, he awoke and looked around the room, disheartened to find his brother already out of his own bed and long gone. Stomach churning, he got dressed as fast as he could and stepped out into the hallway, pausing for a moment to listen. The house was quiet. This was the family routine of late. His siblings either spent their summer nights with friends or made themselves scarce at the break of dawn only to return late at night, to avoid having to deal with their mother.

Nearly friendless, Thomas had no such escape. Sally's family had moved, and she was no longer within walking distance of his house. Not only had she physically moved away from him, but emotionally as well. Still angry and jealous of his relationship with May, she stopped returning his calls, as infrequent as they were.

Thomas hadn't had the nerve to tell Sally that May had

broken up with him. At this point, he didn't think she'd even care. It was the loneliest summer of his life. He had never felt so isolated and forlorn. It caused his head, heart, and stomach to ache all at the same time.

Thomas wandered the neighborhood for hours without aim. At least Sadie was still welcoming and knew of his mother's troubles. She prayed with him and more importantly, fed him. He had known hunger too often in his short life. It coincided with his mother's episodes and his father's absence. Hunger had a profound, debilitating effect on him as a young child. It was a dreaded yet familiar foe as he watched others at school eat, his own stomach screaming in protest.

But he could only spend so much time at Sadie's house. Eventually, he had to return home, never knowing what to expect.

*   *   *

Daytime could be as terrifying as nighttime. At night, horrible things could be softened with dim lighting and shadows. The comfort and escape of sleep was near and realities could be blurred with dreams — perhaps even forgotten.

In the bright light of day, however, there was no hiding anywhere. Every scary scene and image was vivid and unmistakably real. Your eyes didn't play tricks on you during the day. Seeing was believing.

Thomas Paul's palms were sweaty and his head throbbed as he walked up the steps to his front door. He turned the doorknob and crept inside in silence. His breath caught in his throat as he spied her on the sofa.

His mother sat motionless, naked from the waist up. On her lower half she wore only underwear, a blanket tied around her hips. Her large, deflated breasts sagged down almost to her navel, and her skin was pale and dry. Her hair was a frizzy, mangled mess having been brushed out of a beehive up-do. It stuck up and out in all directions, like something Thomas had seen spoofed on TV.

She stared off into space and chewed something in slow, rhythmic bites. Anacin. She often ate it like candy to help with her aches and pains. Aspirin and pure caffeine, mixed with everything and anything else that was prescribed to her. As she crushed the dry tablets between her teeth, without anything to wash them down, her saliva dissolved them, creating a gritty paste that caused her to foam at the mouth.

Her eyes were void of all expression.

Thomas stood in front of her, afraid to move. Where was everybody? He heard a thump from somewhere upstairs, and it made him jump. This in turn startled his mother, and she began to speak but made no sense at all. Her words were a jumble and her voice was panicked and shrill. She grew more and more agitated with every second, and although she stared Thomas straight in the eyes, she seemed to look right through him. Suddenly, she stood up, threw her head back, and smoothed out the blanket with grandiose movements, as if it were the billowing train of a ball gown. As she stood, Thomas could see that her underwear was soiled.

"I'm going home," she said in a frantic voice, reaching across the coffee table, grabbing at something that wasn't there and muttering over and over: "where is my purse…I can't find my purse, somebody stole my purse."

Thomas backed away; terrified she would approach him in

her crazed nakedness. Instead, she merely wandered about the room mumbling before collapsing on the sofa. Thomas stared at her and then, in a desperate attempt to stop her, he turned the dial on the thermostat as high as it would go—naively hoping it would catch the house on fire. He ran outside, screaming as he made his way down the street. It was more than he could handle, and he wanted her gone. He hoped she would burn alive. This awful thing had taken over his mother's body and mind—just like in the movie. Could it really be happening?

The air was hot and dry—suffocating. He heard footsteps on his heels and felt someone's arms reach around him. No! She had caught him. His juvenile attempt at arson and murder had failed.

"Tommy! Stop!" his brother yelled in his ear.

"No! Lemme go!" Thomas fought, deaf to anything around him.

"It's me, Thomas! Stop." His brother was panting as he gripped his arm to keep him from running away. Peter had come down the stairs, spotted their mother and saw Thomas run out the door.

Thomas fell to his knees and sobbed on the pavement.

"It'll be okay. She's just sick. I promise she will get better. Come back inside." He held his hand out for Thomas to grab and help himself up.

Thomas shook his head and looked away. He didn't want to go back there. He wanted to go back to when he was small and his mother was beautiful. He wanted her to smell like soft perfume again, not rancid and sour like she smelled now. He wanted to go back to when he was loved. Back to when his father and mother were happy, but that seemed so long ago.

The daily stress from her long sustained unhappiness played a key role in contributing to the demise of her mental and physical health. All Thomas Paul knew was that she had not really been stable since her operation. The cycle of guilt, unhappiness, stress, anxiety, depression, and pills was now in full swing and was building momentum as the years passed.

She went away again, this time for six weeks. The doctors made their evaluation and determined that she had a chemical imbalance, which was becoming progressively more difficult to control. She suffered from periodic 'psychotic breaks' that caused her irrational behavior and memory lapses. Thomas Paul's mother would call them *blackouts*. Most of her time in the hospital was spent adjusting her increasing litany of medications — always a pill for everything.

It would be years before they tested her ovaries and discovered that they had likely not functioned for a long time, the significance of this combined with her chemical imbalance was not yet clear. Hormone treatment was a new medical practice, which only meant more pills. She had long been buried under an avalanche of learned and practiced mood disorders combined with prescription drug use. She couldn't dig her way out. The cycle continued.

When she came home, once again a sense of normalcy returned to the Stanton household. Whatever that was.

The Stanton family wanted to be normal. They tried to be like any other good, loving, all-American, Catholic family. There were many happy times over the years. Christmas, Easter and Thanksgiving were the most beloved and anticipated holidays, and the family celebrated them in lavish, traditional fashion.

There were also large, extended-family parties, graduations, weddings, baptisms and other holy sacraments. Summer cookouts were fun-filled with boisterous cousins, aunts, and uncles and devoted grandparents who doted on him. He relished the fun he had with his numerous cousins. Thankfully, no audition was required to be accepted and loved by family.

Only they didn't last long enough. When the parties were over and they were alone again, hidden within the confines of their small home, their father would revert back to his true nature — an impatient, violent man, unable to control his rampages. Their mother, once the guests had vanished, would lose her feigned control over her emotional and mental stability.

Unfortunately, there just weren't enough special occasions and holidays in the calendar to counterbalance the painful effects of their parents' volatility.

The dysfunction was inevitable, and Thomas Paul and his siblings were again left adrift in an ocean of forgotten neglect— their mother left as captain, barely clinging to her stability.

There were no lifelines on the horizon.

Chapter 7

"I think I love you, Tommy." Sally stroked his face as they sat on the couch in her basement.

"I think I love you, too," he answered. He truly did love her. He had loved her since the first grade, and he was sure he always would. She kissed him again, their tongues twirling as they explored each other's body over their clothes.

They had reconnected a few months earlier at a wedding. He was on the dance floor with his siblings and his cousins, dancing like fools, when he spotted her across the room. Her back was turned. She wore an emerald-green dress, and her long, lustrous dark auburn hair, curled for the occasion, tumbled down her back. His breath caught in his throat. Could it be? What was she doing here? He left the dance floor and approached her. He tapped her on the shoulder, and she turned and smiled at him.

"I've been watching you, waiting for you to notice me," she said.

He hadn't realized just how much he had missed her. "What are you doing here?"

"The groom is my dad's second cousin." They laughed.

She took him in her arms and squeezed him. He hugged her back. *Sally.* All felt right with the world again.

"I heard about your mom," she said.

"She's better now."

"I'm sorry about you and May."

He waved his hand in the air. "It's all for the best."

"Well, you wanna dance?" she asked.

They had been a couple ever since that night.

Still somewhat shy, even after hours upon hours of make out sessions, Thomas reached up and put a tentative hand on her breast. It felt so nice to touch her and every time he did, it thrilled him just like it had the first time. She gasped but continued kissing him, and he was thankful the lights were dim so she couldn't see him blush.

Sally let her own hand travel up his thigh. He could feel his pulse quicken as her fingers stroked him. Before long, he was fully aroused, and Sally pulled him down so that he was lying on top of her. She wrapped her legs around him and pulled him close.

They rocked and gyrated together in unison on the old sofa, and Thomas Paul's mind began to wander.

He was walking home with his sister, by the drainage ditch, where all the neighborhood kids played. A group of boys came up and started following them.

"Hey, it's Sissy Stanton!" a boy named Billy said. The rest of the boys laughed, and Thomas picked up his pace.

"Thomas, remember what Daddy said?" Anne Marie caught up to *him and grabbed his arm, trying to slow him down.*

Of course he remembered. He had told Thomas that if he didn't start standing up for himself he would be in trouble.

"Are you a boy or a girl, sissy?" Billy continued. *The others laughed louder and joined in the taunting. Thomas could hear them jeering as he ran home.*

When they reached the house, he ran inside and up to his room as Anne Marie blurted out to their father that Thomas had run from the bullies. Within seconds, his father was in his room and dragging him by the arm, back down the stairs and out into the street.

"You listen to me! You are going back there to fight that little bastard and if you lose, I will drag you home and beat the shit out of you again, you got that...Paulina?"

The second demeaning nickname, now saddled upon him by his own father, stung even more than the first. Paulina?

Thomas Paul's eyes widened with fear as his father pushed him ahead on the sidewalk, towards the ditch. They neared the gang of boys, and he could see they were startled to see his father following behind. Maybe they would get scared and leave, Thomas hoped.

His father turned to Anne-Marie, who had followed them back to the site.

"Which one is he?" His words were slow and deliberate.

The boys stood still, not breathing, a touch of fear creeping onto their faces.

Anne-Marie pointed a shaky finger at Billy.

Thomas winced as he felt the hard pinch of his father's strong fingers around the nape of his neck. His father marched him over to Billy and the other boys cleared out of the way.

The group of kids still wasn't quite sure what they were witnessing. They looked at Thomas Paul's father, waiting for him to make his next move. He shoved Thomas at Billy and they both fell to the ground, then he stood back and crossed his arms, the sneer on his face saying it all — the man wanted his son to fight and Billy was more than happy to oblige.

Thomas landed on his back but before he could get up, Billy jumped up and straddled him, pinned him to the ground and punched him in the face. The pain was instant. He closed his eyes and tried to push the boy off his chest while people shouted all around him.

"Hit him!"

"Kick his ass!"

"Sissy can't fight!"

Thomas bucked his hips and tried to shove Billy off but it was futile; the bully was heavier and stronger. Thomas raised his arms to shield his face and try to dodge the hard blows to his head.

Please, he thought to himself. Somebody, help me! He looked around with wild eyes and saw his sister standing by helplessly, a look of horrified guilt on her face. Then he saw his father. He was enraged, almost unrecognizable. Their eyes met, and Thomas offered him a silent plea. Please, Daddy, help me. His father lowered himself down onto the ground, and Thomas felt a wave of enormous relief. Finally, he thought. But instead of helping him, his father knelt right next to him until their faces were inches apart and their eyes were at a level gaze, pounding his fist into the ground, screaming. "Hit him back goddamnit! Hit him back or I'm going to beat your ass when we get home!" Spittle was flying and dribbling from his mouth as he yelled.

His father's words only encouraged Billy to punch harder. "Even your own dad thinks you're a sissy, Stanton," he said with a wicked smile. The others were doubled over with laughter.

Thomas Paul kept his arms up over his face, not to continue shielding himself but so that nobody could see his tears and hear his sobs.

It was true. Nobody liked him, even his own father. He was numb to the punches now, but he would never be numb to the hatred of others.

"How could you humiliate me like that?" his father asked him once they had returned home. His fury had morphed into a sinister calm.

Thomas stared at the floor. The irony of the question wouldn't be clear to him for years.

His father whipped off his belt, and Thomas leaned over the stool without being asked. Even the pain from this second beating, and the memory of this day, didn't compare to the anguish he felt with the repeated use of the new nickname his father saddled him with that day. Paulina. It would become a common name that his siblings adopted for him when they were taunting and teasing him. He despised it.

Sally ran her fingers through his hair, and her touch jolted him back to reality. He stopped kissing her for a moment and looked at her. Sweet Sally. She smiled up at him, and he touched his lips to hers again. He wished they could see him, all of them, he thought to himself. There was nothing 'sissy' about what he was doing now—making out with his girlfriend. His father would be happy, of that he was certain. Sally rolled him over onto his back so that she was straddling him on the couch. She reached up and peeled her shirt off over her head and tossed it to the floor.

"Take your shirt off," she said, helping him.

Thomas fumbled and twisted to remove his own shirt, tossing it to the floor like she had done with her own. Sally lowered herself on top of him, and the sensation of her warmth against his bare skin was electrifying. They groped and kissed each other again but Thomas hesitated. *How could he still be so clueless about something so primal?* He was afraid and unsure about how to continue. *Was she really ready to go all the way?*

Sensing his hesitation, Sally reached down in a clumsy attempt to unfasten his jeans, and as she lifted her hips to inch them down, they heard a door slam upstairs.

"Shit!" she said as she pushed him to the floor.

Oh God! Thomas thought as he pulled his clothes back on. *Will I ever figure this out?*

After a sheepish, awkward goodbye to Sally's mother, Thomas Paul walked all the way home, refusing a ride so that he could calm the raging teenage blood still racing through his veins. He opened the door to the house and was surprised to find his mother awake, sitting, hunched over in her chair, smoking. All impure thoughts of Sally vanished at the sight of his mother, looking disheveled but mostly alert.

"Hi, Thomas Paul," she said, her voice void of emotion.

"Hi," he said.

"Come sit with me," she beckoned.

He sat on the sofa and looked down at the coffee table, littered with piles of wet, mucus-filled tissues.

"Honey, do me a favor, will you? Take my glass and get me some water. Don't forget to fill it up with ice. And get my pills for me, please."

Thomas headed for the bathroom.

"Which ones?"

"The red one, the blue one, and two of the white ones," she replied.

"What about the yellow one?"

"No, that one I take before bed with the other ones," his mother answered.

He walked back into the room and held his hand out to her. She took the pills from him and swallowed them.

"Take Mommy's dirty Kleenexes and throw them away for me, please?" she whined.

Thomas had to force himself not to shudder at the touch and feel of her wet, slimy tissues. As he picked them up, she was wracked with another coughing fit and filled another one with her thick, warm sputum — a nasty symptom of her emphysema. Thomas stifled a gag. Just hurry and pick them up and then get out of here, he thought to himself. As he gathered up the last few tissues, he saw it. It had been hidden underneath the mound of disgust. He stared at it. The hairbrush. He knew what was coming.

He walked into the other room to dispose of the tissues, hoping she would let him escape.

"How was school?" she asked.

No such luck. He returned to sit with her.

He shrugged. "The usual. Nobody likes me."

"Oh, honey. I wish there was something I could do to help you," she sighed. "If only you liked sports."

Thomas rolled his eyes. Sports! Even from her.

"I went to Sally's," he said, eager to change the subject.

"I like that Sally. What a pretty girl. You two get along so well—you always have." She blew a puff of smoke into the air again.

Neither one of them spoke for a moment; the only sound was his mother's raspy exhales. The room was growing cloudy.

"Honey…"

He froze.

"Brush Mommy's hair for me, would you?"

His heart sank. It was one of those things that she regularly insisted be done for her. It seemed to Thomas that he was always the only one around on those days when she emerged from her bed, awake and lucid, requesting to be groomed. Or perhaps she just preferred his technique to the others'. Either way, it was an agonizing chore and no way to escape doing it. First the tissues and now this!

"Please, Thomas Paul, I just can't do it myself, and it feels so nice when you do," she cajoled.

Thomas took the brush in his hand and straddled her behind the sofa. He steeled himself for what was to follow.

Her hair was a nest—a greasy, unwashed, unkempt mess of tangles. Weeks earlier, it had been a stylish beehive, teased, pinned and sprayed, high and shiny on her head. It hadn't been combed or washed since then, and it was now his job to remove all the pins that held it in place and brush it out smooth.

Thomas removed all the pins and with a shudder started brushing, trying his best not to pull too hard. Sitting this close to her, he could smell her. She had the odor of someone sickly masked with the heavy stench of cigarette smoke. She seldom brushed her teeth but when she did, she used Ajax and peroxide but couldn't seem to realize that this did nothing good for her teeth or her breath.

She didn't bathe or wash her hair when his father was away because she was simply too lazy and depressed. Her mind was filled with too many other thoughts. Thoughts that were too complex and confusing for anyone else to comprehend. Thoughts that were more important than the day-to-day needs of her children or even herself. All Thomas knew right now was that she smelled bad, and he longed for the days when a hug from her would fill his nose with the sweet essence of White Shoulders perfume.

No matter how hard he tried, he couldn't avoid touching her hair with his fingers—it was the only way to make some sense of the knots on her head. He grimaced at the feeling of the oil on his hands, unsure of what was worse—the phlegm from her lungs or this. Finally, he could pull the brush through without hitting any snags, and he let the rhythm of the strokes lull his mind elsewhere — back to Sally.

Sex, lust, fornication, and sin—the thought of Sally's body and her unapologetic desire made him almost dizzy, until the guilt of it all scared him sober. He stopped brushing. He needed to get away.

"Oh, please, Thomas Paul. Brush it some more. Mommy is so tired from doing for everyone else. I just don't get to do anything for myself. Please keep brushing."

He wanted to whip the stinking brush across the room and scream. He prayed for his sister to walk through the door, anything to relieve him from this hellish duty.

He brushed and she smoked.

His thoughts drifted to God.

"Mom, how come you never come to church with us?"

"Oh, Thomas Paul, you know how I feel about the church." She put out her cigarette in a glass ashtray, filled to the brim with butts that had been sucked down to the filters.

He did know some things. She was angry that the church wouldn't allow birth control and that they had so many rules. Rules she couldn't follow.

"Remember? I've told you before. I've sinned so much there isn't enough forgiveness for the things I've done."

That was her standard answer to the church question but he still didn't really understand what she meant. As if sensing his confusion, she sat up straight and turned around to face him.

In a shameless, matter-of-fact tone she announced, "Thomas Paul, neither you nor your little sister belong to your daddy." She waited.

His mouth dropped open, but no sound came out. He was surprised at this news but, even at his young age of fourteen, he wasn't shocked. She had had several boyfriends in the past, years before, when his father was away. Lots of them. The foggy memories came flooding back as he sat behind her.

She gestured for him to resume the brushing. "Your daddy's name was Bruno Morelli, and your sister's daddy was a man named Bobby. You know Bobby. He works at the hardware store downtown, but I don't like to go there anymore. I don't want him to see me when I'm sick. And I'm fat now, not like when we were together."

Thomas kept brushing. He worried if he quit she would stop talking.

"Your real father was in the military, stationed at the base not far from here. He was older. He told me he couldn't have children." She lit another cigarette, filling the air with a fresh cloud of smoke.

"When I found out I was pregnant with you, I knew you weren't your daddy's because he wasn't home when you were conceived. But I stopped seeing Bruno and never told him about you. You look just like him."

She was overcome with a coughing spasm, but Thomas Paul was so entranced by her story that he didn't even flinch when she hacked and spat into yet another tissue and tossed it onto the coffee table. His thoughts ran in all directions. He hated his father but more than anything in the world, he wanted to be loved by him. This newfound revelation changed nothing and yet changed everything. His 'daddy' was and always would be the man who raised him, but something about this news made him almost happy. He believed that his real father would love him, truly love him, without question or condition.

A fantasy slowly formed in his mind—a stranger, seeing his son for the first time, his eyes lighting up when he realized that this boy was his mirror image.

His mother turned around again and fixed her eyes on him. "Thomas Paul, you better never, never, never, ever tell your daddy. He would kill me if he ever found out."

Thomas Paul swallowed and stared back at her. He had once seen his father, red-faced and crazed with fury, with his hands around his mother's neck, lifting her off the ground and pinning her up against the wall, her feet dangling—choking her over a credit-card bill while their children watched helplessly at the dinner table. Anne Marie had thrown herself at him, screaming for him to stop strangling the life out of their mother. Caught off guard, he released his grip on her throat, and she slumped to the floor.

Thomas knew that his mother was right, that knowing the true paternity of his two youngest children would send his father over the edge. With this scandalous disclosure, he also knew that his mother hated his daddy, too. She had no love for him anymore, and she blamed him for everything that was wrong in her life. She was helpless to stand up to him, but she had hurt him today without his knowing.

In silence, he nodded his head as a solemn promise to keep their secret. After a while she got up, lit another cigarette, and headed for the kitchen. He didn't know what had come over her that day. What had made her decide to share this revelation with him? His mother hadn't seemed this clear and focused in a long time, and he knew that every word she had spoken was the truth. He was filled with curiosity and intrigue.

In the weeks to come, she would try and help Thomas Paul search for Bruno Morelli. Their efforts would ultimately be fruitless but nonetheless, they gave him some much-needed comfort and escape, if only for a while.

Thomas Paul put the brush down, still trying to process this information.

"Oh, and guess what?" his mother said. "The secretary from St. Martha's called. You got the job at Camp Evergreen this summer."

Thomas Paul jumped up from the couch, ecstatic. "Oh my God, really? I get to go back to camp? I've dreamed about this for so long! I can't believe it's really gonna happen."

The day had been an emotional roller-coaster. What could possibly be next?

Chapter 8

1974

Thomas Paul held Sally's hand as they stood in line to board the long yellow school bus for Cincinnati. Other than the occasional family weekends at his grandparent's cabin in the summer, this was to be his first trip out of town. On his own, no less, with his beautiful girlfriend. It was a Spanish-class field trip, organized by Sally's school, and since Thomas Paul took Spanish at his own school, he was allowed to join the group. His parents were happy to see him go, as well. Glad that he was finally out doing fun things with others, and with a girl. They were fine with paying the small fee for his trip.

They boarded the bus and made their way toward the dark green, vinyl benches at the back. Thomas slid into the first available bench, snagging a coveted window seat, and Sally followed beside him. For the next few minutes, Thomas gazed out the window and watched other students climb aboard. Every face was that of a stranger, and he welcomed the anonymity of being from a different school. It was like he was the new kid in class.

"Hey, Tony," Sally said as she waved a boy over and gestured for him to sit near them. Thomas Paul turned his head at the sound of Sally's voice.

"Tony, this is my boyfriend, Tommy."

Tony nodded his head and smiled as he moved into the bench directly in front of them, leaning his back against the window then turning to face them.

"Hey, man," Tony said.

"Hey," Thomas answered and smiled.

Tony White was a new friend of Sally's from her new school. He had pale, clear skin and wavy, wiry, sandy blonde hair. He was of medium height and thick, though not fat. Beefy. He wore skin-tight Levis, as was fashionable. Tony propped his arm over the back of the seat and spent the entire trip to Cincinnati turned around, talking and laughing with Sally and Thomas.

The three of them spent the whole day hanging out together, and Tony treated Thomas like a buddy, one of the guys, as if they had known each other for years. Sally was pleased the two got along so well and that there was no jealousy simmering below the surface between the two boys. What she didn't know and never would have imagined was that in the space of one day, her boyfriend had fallen hopelessly, madly, in love with Tony White.

The feeling had struck him like a hammer when he first laid eyes on Tony. It was love at first sight. His mouth dried up and remained that way the entire day as he stared at Tony's body in the skin-tight jeans, anxious and confused that he found himself fantasizing about what he would look like naked.

In the close proximity of the bus, Thomas Paul's senses became overloaded with everything about Tony. He was even keenly aware of his scent and breathed it in deeply all day, intoxicated by the aroma now imprinted in his memory — a mix of fresh laundry and musty teenage hair. Tony's kindness towards him only deepened Thomas Paul's growing infatuation. Thankfully, as Thomas was naturally shy, it helped to disguise his obsession. He appeared normal, perhaps a bit aloof, even though his heart raced and something inside him burned and made his stomach churn. It was painful and pleasurable at the same time. Thomas was both elated and traumatized at the feelings he was experiencing. He couldn't explain or understand what was happening to him. *Muy caliente.* It was the only piece of Spanish that he had retained all day.

As they rode the bus home that night, Sally leaned over in the darkness and kissed Thomas for a few minutes. He closed his eyes and couldn't help imagining he was kissing Tony. Later, while Sally rested her head on his shoulder and slept, Thomas stared at the back of Tony's head. Tony was leaning back in his seat, asleep, his head bouncing and rolling back and forth with the intermittent, jerking movements of the bus.

As the other kids slept, Thomas let his mind wander. He had seen many naked boys before: his older brother and some of the neighborhood kids, during sleepovers, camp outs, or playing 'doctor'—seemingly innocent experiences. But as he sat on the bus, he could think of nothing else except what it would be like to be naked with Tony White, touching one another in ways that he had only touched a girl before. Dim moonlight shone through the bus windows. Thomas held his breath and ever so slowly, so as not to be noticed, he reached up and touched Tony's hair. A lump formed in his throat and warm tears clouded his eyes at the thought of the trip ending and having to separate from him. As the bus rumbled along, Tony's head jostled again, and Thomas quickly pulled his hand away.

His fear would be more than realized. Once they were home and each went their separate ways, he would never see Tony again but would remember him, as clear as day, for the rest of his life.

After a few long, tortured weeks spent doing nothing but going through the motions of his daily routine, Thomas Paul refused to get out of bed. His mother was worried. His anguish had become impossible to hide.

"You're depressed, honey. I can see it. I know about these things, and I'm taking you to see my doctor."

That afternoon, Thomas returned home with a prescription for Sinequan®—a mood elevator, just like the ones his mother took. He swallowed the first twenty-five milligram pill, flopped down on his bed, pulled the covers over his head, and waited. He knew he could never be with Tony White and was tormented that he even desired such a thing. If these little pills could take away the pain from those crushing realizations, he was ready.

But Tony White had a hold over him that apparently no benzodiazepine could cure. His heart still ached. He was sick with longing for Tony and disgusted with himself for those very feelings. *It is an abomination for a man to lie with another man.* The scripture repeated over and over in his mind.

He could not accept his desire for something so sinful and wrong, no matter how good it felt to him. He would surely spend eternity burning in hell if he could not find a way to crush these feelings.

"What's wrong, Tommy?" Sally asked him, as they sat together in her basement.

"What do you mean?"

"You're acting weird. You seem so far away all the time — you hardly even want to make-out anymore." Her voice was tinged with frustration.

Thomas shrugged.

"There are other boys, you know."

Thomas stiffened. Other boys?

"Other guys who want to take me out."

"No, Sally. I love you. Only you." He did love her. He couldn't lose her.

"So, you don't like somebody else?" She searched his face for answers.

Thomas Paul's mouth dropped open. "No, Sally. Never! Of course not." He took her hand in his own. "You said 'other guys.' Do you want to date other guys? Like...Tony?" Just saying his name made Thomas Paul's heart flutter.

"Tony? No! He's like a brother to me."

"Do you see him around school a lot?" Thomas continued. His tone had changed from mild jealousy to genuine interest.

"Sure." She shrugged. "Of course."

"The three of us should hang out sometime," Thomas offered.

"I'm telling you that I'm worried about your feelings for me and all you want to talk about is hanging out with the guys?"

Sally looked at him, saying nothing for a moment.

Her eyes began to water, and she got up from the couch. She walked over to the desk and opened a drawer. She had a photo in her hand when she sat back down on the couch and held it up for Thomas to look at.

It was a photo of him, at school, but he had no idea when it had been taken. "What is this?" he asked.

"I've been in love with you since the first grade." She sniffled. "When I had to transfer schools, I kept in touch with Sharon Fields from time to time. She worked on the yearbook committee."

Thomas waited, confused.

"I asked her to watch for pictures of you and paid her to keep them for me." She blushed and started to laugh. "Five bucks."

"I don't understand," Thomas said.

"I love you so much. But you don't love me the same way."

Thomas shook his head and started to worry. "What do you mean?"

"There's been something going on with you for a while and I'm not sure what it is. Ever since we got back from Cincinnati ,you've been different. I think we need to take a break."

Thomas was speechless. Could she have known? "Sally, please, no … I don't want to break up."

She kissed him on the cheek. "You are still the most beautiful boy I have ever seen. I will love you and your blue eyes forever no matter what happens." Thomas curled up on his bed and cried. How could he blame her? His heart was broken. He had lost the girl and the boy he loved, in one fell swoop. He was overcome with sadness and guilt.

Thomas Paul thought about it for days. He was convinced that if one pill knocked him out, surely what was left in the bottle would be enough to kill him. He sneaked into the kitchen, making sure nobody was looking. He took the bottle from the cabinet, coughing as he put it in his pocket to mask the sound of the tablets shaking around in the plastic container. He filled a glass of water and retreated to his room and closed the door. Sitting on the edge of his bed, he counted the pills. There were twenty-two left. He tried to determine how many pills he could swallow at one time and settled on three small piles.

In his mind, he said his goodbyes to his family members and wondered how they would feel when they found his body the next day. Would they miss him? Would they be sad? He took a deep breath, scooped the first pile into his hand, and swallowed it down with ease. He started to cry and for a moment he was scared. But this was the only way to be free from his torment. He swallowed the next handful, and his tears subsided. There was no turning back now. He gulped the third and final handful, drained the water glass, and tossed the empty bottle into his trash can. Soon, he fell into a deep sleep, certain that he would never wake up.

However, the next morning did come and to his shock and disbelief, he awoke. Groggy and dazed, he looked around the room and realized what he'd done. How could he be alive? Scared and more depressed than before, he climbed out of bed, dressed, and made his way to school for the first time in days without telling a soul what he'd done.

"What did you do?" his mother asked him, the empty pill bottle in her hand, as he walked back into the house after school. She was distraught. "I've been so worried. Did you take these, Thomas Paul?"

His eyes widened to see that she had fished the bottle out of the trash can in his room. "Yes." He didn't even bother to lie.

"Oh my God." She stared at him, frantic. "We have to get you to a hospital. We have to get your stomach pumped!" She darted back and forth around the room. "Where are my keys? Oh my God, where are my keys!"

"Mom, stop! I took them all last night. Nothing happened."

"Are you sure? Are you telling me the truth?" She grabbed his shoulders and looked him straight in the eyes. "Why did you take them? Were you trying to kill yourself? Oh God! Oh God! Was it something *I* did?"

"No, Mom. It wasn't you."

His mother started crying and stroked his face. "Well then what, Thomas Paul?" she pleaded as she pushed the hair out of his eyes. "What would make you want to do a thing like that, honey?

Thomas fell silent. Mute. He could not bring himself to confess the true reason to anybody. He had been honest about the attempted suicide, but Tony White would forever remain his own secret.

"Did you ever stop to think what this would do to me?" she cried. "How could I have lived with myself if you had died? You have to promise me you will never do this again."

Thomas Paul started crying. "I promise." But in his mind, he wasn't so sure.

She prodded him one more time. "If it wasn't something I did and it wasn't something your daddy did, what was it?"

"I don't know, Mom. I just don't know."

"Well, we'll keep this between us for now but when

you're ready to talk about things, I want you to come to me. You know I love you, honey, and I would do anything for you."

Before long it was all a blur. Summer was almost here and things were happening. He would soon be starting his first job at camp. The fear from the reality of his suicide attempt had a profound effect on him. He didn't want to live without Sally or

Tony White, but he was still alive.

He rationalized that, obviously, God must have wanted him to live. It had to be the only explanation.

Chapter 9

1975

Thomas Paul could barely contain his excitement as they made the hour-long drive to Camp Evergreen. The camp was nestled in the midst of the 2,600 acres of Beaver Creek Park, stretching along the banks of the Ohio River. He had gone to camp many times as a camper, but this year he would stay for a full six weeks as a 'Blackfoot' —a member of the Mess Hall kitchen staff.

As exciting as it had been to be a camper at Evergreen, being part of the staff was going to be even better, he was sure. Responsibility, authority, autonomy, freedom and, most of all, acceptance as one of the guys—for that Thomas Paul would peel a million potatoes if they asked him. He was thrilled to have been chosen from dozens of young boys clamoring for a spot at the camp.

The sun was high and bright in the sky, just like Thomas Paul's spirit. He peered over the front seat to look down the road, watching for the peeling red arrow on the old, painted, wooden camp sign.

His father, sensing Thomas Paul's enthusiasm asked, "Are you excited, son?"

"Oh yes, sir." It was an understatement, to say the least.

"Well, we hope you have a good time, honey," his mother chimed in.

How could he not? Thomas thought to himself. He was beyond grateful to be heading back to the woods this summer.

Finally, they turned onto the gravel drive and made their way through the park to the campsite.

The camp was similar to thousands of other summer camps throughout the nation. It consisted of small, crude cabins with little or no electricity and basic latrines with toilets. There were showers and a trough for communal hand-washing. Among the other buildings were a mess hall, an infirmary, and a lodge where arts and crafts, religious services, and other activities took place. Outside there was a large fire pit, swimming pool, and ball diamonds spread out within the trees.

Camp Evergreen also had a gong, made from the steel tire of a railroad car. It was rung several times a day to announce various activities. The campers were divided into tribes with authentic Native American names such as Shawnee, Sioux, Seneca, and Cherokee. It was primitive and in the heat of the summer, teeming with young boys of all ages, it was often hot, humid, and buggy. For Thomas Paul it was paradise. There was nowhere else in the whole world he would rather be.

Amidst the tall, majestic trees that cocooned their sanctuary, camp was a place where Thomas almost fit in for the first time in his life. Most of his peers seemed to like him and accept him, or at the very least, tolerate him. He was a bona fide member of the summer brotherhood at Camp Evergreen.

Thomas Paul jumped out of the car as soon as his father eased into a parking spot by the administration building. He grabbed his sleeping bag and small suitcase and waited impatiently for his mother and father to climb out of the car. His mother smiled at his exuberance.

Thomas led the way into the building and was greeted at the entrance by Father Henderson, the Camp director.

"Welcome back, Thomas Paul! We're happy to have you here again with us this summer." He offered a warm smile and held out his hand as he spoke.

Thomas gripped the priest's hand and returned his best handshake, firm and confident, like his father had taught him years before. *A strong man's handshake.*

Father Henderson, who never forgot anyone's name, then turned to Thomas Paul's parents. "John…Carol, always good to see you. How have you been?" They were honored that he remembered them after having only met them briefly once or twice during summers past.

Thomas was pleased that his mother wasn't sick anymore. It was the weekend, his father was home, and therefore his mother was clean, dressed appropriately, and pretty much normal. To anyone else, it appeared that Ward and June Cleaver were happily dropping the Beaver off at camp for the summer. Thomas was relieved.

He stood back and watched his parents exchange small talk with the man who was like a second father to him. Father Henderson was the essence of Camp Evergreen. He was larger than life to all who knew him. He was brilliant, strict, disciplined, and unfaltering in his direction, yet calm, fair, and kind and deeply caring, with a wonderful sense of humor. He loved to laugh and loved what he did. He was what Thomas wanted his father to be —Thomas adored him.

It was the second week of summer. A fresh, young batch of boys had arrived two days before and the camp was bustling non-stop with daily activities. The campers flowed out of the mess hall after lunch and made their way to the lodge for arts-and-crafts time.

Thomas Paul was a natural when it came to anything artistic. He wasn't a counselor so he was free to participate in camp activities during his breaks from meal preparations in the kitchen. Unlike at school, the other boys took notice of his talent in a positive way. The younger ones would ask him for help and direction with their projects, and the older ones would quietly admire his creations.

Thomas Paul could string the yarn around two Popsicle sticks tighter than anyone else; the color schemes of his God's Eye were bright and original. His painting skills were imaginative and clever and though most other boys wouldn't say anything out loud, they took a bit more care and made somewhat of an effort when dragging their own brushes over paper or rocks.

Today, Thomas Paul was concentrating on a Native American dream catcher. He wrapped a long piece of leather around a five-inch hoop, careful not to leave any gaps. He had chosen a few beads and several feathers to string onto his design once the smooth, brown leather was glued in place.

In the corner of the lodge, two boys were fooling around, laughing and teasing one another as they painted small rocks. They flicked their paintbrushes at each other and dissolved into hysterics at the sight of their faces, covered in multicolored dots, like psychedelic chicken pox.

Thomas Paul looked up from his work for a moment. It was Willie and Jim, who were a few years younger than he. He could overhear their banter.

"Check this out," Jim said.

"That looks like shit, man," Willie replied, guffawing at his verbal jab.

"Oh yeah?" In a split second, Jim grabbed Willie's rock and whipped it across the room.

With an audible thump, it struck the forehead of a young boy named David who was working at the table next to Thomas. The boy cried out and raised his hand to his head. Bright crimson blood started to flow from behind his stubby fingers and as the others caught sight of it, they started to panic. The sounds of screaming and the sight of their wide eyes as they stared at him made David become even more hysterical.

Thomas Paul looked around, nonplussed. Without much thought, he hurried next door into the mess hall and returned with a clean dishtowel. The chaos had not lessened and even the counselors stood helpless, wondering what to do. Thomas pushed his way through the crowded room and stood next to David. He removed the boy's hand and covered the deep gash with the towel, applying pressure while he waited for help.

"It'll be okay, David. It's just a small cut," he said.

David stopped screaming for a moment and with tear-filled eyes, looked up at Thomas.

"Cuts on the head just bleed a lot, even if they're not really bad, but you'll be okay," he soothed. He had remembered learning this in school, along with the importance of applying pressure to a bleeding wound.

David's piercing cries slowly turned into breathy, heaving sobs, as he listened to Thomas Paul's words.

Father Henderson made his way through the crowd to find Thomas, unfazed by the drama, doing his best to help amidst the frenzy. Thomas met his eyes, calm but eager for further instruction, and for a split second he saw something on Father's face he had rarely, if ever, seen before.

"Well, you're the only one here with a calm head."

Thomas offered a half-smile and shrugged. The reality was that in his home, the days were frequently filled with chaos. It was by no means normal but it was *the norm,* and it was always expected. Between his mother's physical and mental health and his father's moods, a rock to the forehead was no big deal. A rock to the head had reason and rhyme, it had a real cause and a tangible effect, it would be healed, and the scar that it would leave would be external. Thomas knew from experience that those were much less painful than the internal ones.

Father removed the towel from David's head and studied the wound, the blood flow having slowed from gushing to a trickle. "Stitches," he sighed.

"Thomas, I can't leave the camp, and the counselors must stay with their charges. Do you know how to drive yet?" His tone, as always, was firm and even.

Thomas Paul nodded in silence, but his heart began to race a little.

"Can you drive a stick shift?" Father asked.

He hesitated but reasoned that this wasn't the best time to lie to a priest. "No."

Father shook his head, removed the lanyard from around his neck, and thrust the keys at Thomas Paul. "Just get in the car. Be careful and you will be fine." He looked at the injured boy, his sobs now lulled to sporadic whimpers. David's younger brother had pushed through the jumble of boys and stood next to him with his mouth wide. "Michael, you go with them. Hold the towel on your brother's head while Thomas drives you to the hospital. It'll be fine." He patted the boy on the back and gave them all a thumbs-up.

Father Henderson drove a deep blue 1968 Chevy Nova. David and Michael climbed into the back seat, the vinyl warm from the summer sun. David's gash was still slightly oozing from behind the Band-Aid Father had applied for the journey to the clinic in Williamsburg. Thomas Paul lowered himself into the driver's seat, slammed the door, and thrust the massive clutch to the floor as Father had instructed him and started the ignition — much to the awe of every camper and counselor watching the scene unfold.

Clutch down, shift gear, ease off clutch, give gas. Clutch down, shift gear, ease off clutch, give gas. He repeated the mantra over and over in his head as the car rumbled beneath him. How hard could this be? He was exhilarated with the new task assigned to him. The responsibility. Driving alone, a stick shift to boot! Father Henderson's very own car. Everyone watching!

The adrenaline rushed through his veins as the Nova jolted ahead, jerking the boys back and forth. Thomas Paul had driven his father's car several times, but the Chevy was a very different beast. It was a behemoth to shift, steer, and control. He was frightened but determined not to let anyone down.

"Hold on, guys, everything's going to be fine!" Thomas Paul laughed as he stepped on the gas pedal to smooth out the ride and avoid stalling the engine. He steered the car out of the parking lot towards the camp exit and then made his way up and down the hills of the long, winding park roads. Thankfully the traffic was light and nobody was around to witness the few times he indeed stalled the car.

The drive on the highway was easier and downright thrilling. The windows were rolled down and the wind cooled their faces in the mid-summer heat. Thomas Paul was tall for his age, strong and fit, and could easily pass for a boy of seventeen or eighteen. To anyone passing by, a glance in the Chevy would show nothing out of the ordinary. Just a handsome young man, tanned and muscular in a tank top, with his blond hair blowing wildly in the wind, taking his little brothers fishing, perhaps. Behind the wheel of the car, Thomas Paul felt like someone else. He felt older, in control, cool, maybe even envied a bit by those who had stayed behind in a girlish panic. *Thomas Paul to the rescue!* It would be a ride he would never forget.

Several hours later, Thomas, Michael, and David, now with eight fresh stitches on his noggin', returned, car transmission intact, to a small crowd of cheering campers and counselors. Father Henderson stood in the front of the motley group and smiled at Thomas Paul with the same look on his face from hours before. It was pride.

Thomas felt something grow inside him. It was almost funny that it had been nothing more than a rock, tossed haphazardly with boyish mischief. A simple rock had helped to restore his almost non-existent self–confidence — the confidence that through the years had been slowly stripped away from him.

Today, he was a hero, and it felt better than he could ever have imagined.

Chapter 10

"Father Bob's coming today! Did you hear? Father Bob's coming.

"Father Bob? Yeah. Cool—who is Father Bob?"

"Don't you know Father Bob?" As the weekend approached, there was a buzz around camp among the counselors and some of the campers about the impending arrival of the mysterious Father Bob. It was the first Thomas had heard of the new priest but it was evident the man was loved and adored by all who knew him. Thomas was curious to meet the much-talked-about stranger.

That afternoon, everyone was gathered at the pool. They screamed, laughed, and splashed about in the hot sun, not a care in the world. Thomas Paul placed his beach towel on the concrete deck, next to the lifeguard chair. He sat back and soaked up the rays, the intermittent splashes from the pool cooling his hot, brown skin.

"Hey, Tommy."

Thomas squinted and looked up for the source of the voice.

"Hey, Randy," he said to the lifeguard. His actual name was Andy Pierce. 'Randy' was nineteen years old and had been the lifeguard at Evergreen for the past two years. He was tall and fit, like Thomas, but with dark eyes and black hair, which he kept shorter to keep him cooler while he roasted in the sun all day. He was perched up in the lifeguard's chair, his body dark and slick with suntan oil. Randy was friendly, and Thomas Paul found him easy to talk to.

He turned his eyes back to the pool but felt Randy still looking at him.

"You must have a lot of girlfriends, huh?" Randy asked him, out of the blue.

Thomas shrugged, unsure of what to say. He'd had girlfriends but hadn't actually 'had pussy' yet. Randy loved to talk about pussy and girls in general, which saddled him with the nickname of 'Randy Andy' that eventually turned into simply Randy.

Most of the guys talked about girls a lot, what they'd done, what they wanted and hoped to do someday soon. Thomas did his best to laugh and go along with the conversations. In reality, most girls, even Sally, intimidated him. His body responded to them but he had yet to go all the way with any of them, much to his and their frustration.

"You're a great-looking guy. I even notice the dudes here staring you up and down," Randy continued. "Don't get any wise ideas though, man," he laughed. "No fags here."

Thomas noticed it, too, the looks from other boys. He just never knew what they were thinking. His appearance felt more like a curse than an asset. *You're as pretty as a girl, Thomas Paul.*

You should've been born a girl. You're too pretty to be a boy. People looked at him and were drawn to him, but the attention often seemed to work against him once they got to know him better. He wished he could just blend in.

"Are you gay, Tommy?" Randy asked, matter-of-factly.

Thomas was stunned by the question and by Randy's directness. The image of Tony White in his tight jeans flashed through his mind, and his stomach twisted into a knot. It took a few seconds for him to answer, the shock evident on his face.

"No way, I have a girlfriend. Her name is Sally," he lied. Now wasn't the time to admit that she had actually broken up with him. But gay? He wasn't gay, he thought to himself. Is that what others thought of him? He wasn't even really sure what 'gay' was, but he knew that people hated queers, and he was most certainly not a queer.

"Oh yeah? Cool. Is she hot?" Randy leaned forward, a smile on his face, eager for details about Sally. He kept his eyes trained on the swimmers in the water while he waited for Thomas to answer.

"Yeah. She's a redhead," he said, not quite knowing what else he should share.

Randy nodded and smiled. "Tits?" he asked and waited.

Impatient with Thomas Paul's confusion, he stopped watching the pool, looked Thomas in the eye, and held up his hands like he was holding an invisible baseball in each one. "Tits, Tommy! She got 'em? Big? Small? You been to second base with her?"

Thomas laughed out loud. "Yeah, they're big … and round." He looked away. "And soft I touch them all the time…she loves it." She had loved it and was willing to let him touch them and kiss them as much as he wanted. Thinking of her now and talking about her body made him yearn for her. He wondered what she was doing while he spent his days at Evergreen.

"Nice." Randy smiled and leaned back in his chair, turning his attention back to the swimmers "I don't even know her and my dick's getting hard thinking about her. No offense, man." He laughed and swung his whistle around on his finger, the black cord whipping quick circles in one direction, then the other.

Thomas wasn't offended at all. Randy was a nice guy, and he didn't know many nice guys. Not truly nice ones, like Randy appeared to be. Still, Thomas was anxious to change the subject. He didn't want Randy to start asking him about the rest of Sally's body parts and inquire just what he had done and not done with her — or find out how he had been too clueless to go all the way with her.

"So, who's this Father Bob that everyone's been talking about?" Thomas asked.

Randy leaned forward again. "Oh, Father Bob's great, man. He's a priest and all but you'd never know it. When he's not leading service, it's like he's one of us. Fits right in."

"Where's he from?" Thomas continued.

"He's the parish priest at St. Bartholomew's, I think."

"How long is he gonna stay?"

"Dunno. Probably just the weekend, I guess. That's what he usually does. He comes a few times every summer. Always does something cool when he's here...plays pranks and jokes and shit like that...you'll see."

His curiosity somewhat satisfied and sweat now dripping down his back from the heat, Thomas Paul decided that this was the perfect time to get into the water. "I'm getting in," he announced. He stood up and started walking towards the diving board.

Swimming was something he was good at and it showed as he sauntered out onto the board, just as his mother had taught him, and executed a clean, polished dive with barely a splash. In an instant he surfaced and hoisted himself out with grace and ease. Dripping but refreshed, he waited in line again for another turn on the board.

Then suddenly, from out of nowhere, they heard a loud siren, like a police car or ambulance, approaching. As the screeching grew closer, the entire body of swimmers stopped rough-housing and came to near silence. Thomas squinted in the sunlight and looked towards the road. Like something he would see in a movie, a four-door sedan drove up the gravel road and came to halt in a cloud of dust, directly in front of the pool's gate.

A bright red light atop the car blinked and flashed as the siren blared on, announcing the arrival of Camp Evergreen's esteemed new guest. He stepped out of the car, bigger than life, to greet a small gathering of campers and counselors clamoring to welcome him into their sacred summer haven.

Father Stumpf scanned the pool area and waved to everyone. Thomas Paul, still standing by the diving board, held up his hand to shield his eyes from the sun and get a better look at the newcomer. For a few seconds their eyes met, and Father Stumpf smiled at him, showing gleaming, straight, white teeth. Thomas offered an awkward wave and dove back into the pool. He swam around the water and tried not to be obvious as he watched Father walk around and greet dozens of boys, many of whom he called by their first names.

The next evening, Father Stumpf, dressed in customary church robes, presided over the weekly Friday-night service. When it was Thomas Paul's turn to receive communion, he detected a slight smile on the priest's face, as if he recognized him from the day before, even though he was now clothed and no longer soaking wet.

Saturday evening, after all campers had departed for home and the staff awaited the spry new batch due to arrive the next morning—the time for tomfoolery amongst the counselors who stayed on all weekend. On those nights, under the cover of darkness, a ritualistic rite of passage would take place, enjoyed by all at some point during the summer—skinny-dipping at the pool.

Liberated from their duties for one evening each week, the staff let loose. They hooted and hollered as they dove, splashed, and dunked one another under the stars. There were chicken fights and races across the pool, raunchy gestures and foul-mouthed language—young teenage men in their unsupervised glory, as naked as God had made them.

"Hey!" someone shouted.

Several boys stopped splashing and looked around as Randy strolled out onto the diving board, his dick dangling and bouncing to and fro with each step.

"It's been too long, boys. I ain't seen any pussy in a month!" He bounced lightly on the board as he spoke.

Many in the crowd laughed and shouted in agreement.

"So…" reaching down to grab his now semi-erect penis with one hand, "which one of you wants to suck my dick?" The group jeered.

"In your dreams, Pierce!"

"You wish!"

"You gotta suck mine first!"

Randy howled like a wolf as he jumped as high as he could, executed a front flip then clasped his knees to his chest and plunged into the water, starting a cannonball contest amongst the others.

Despite the horseplay and craziness in the moonlight, Thomas could feel he was being watched.

"You're Thomas Paul, aren't you?" Father Bob was behind him in the water.

He knows my name, Thomas thought to himself. He turned around and nodded, thankful it was dark, his nervousness hopefully hidden from the imposing man.

"You're quite a swimmer," the priest continued.

"Thanks." Thomas couldn't believe Father was skinny-dipping with them. Seeing him in his robes on Friday night, solemn and reverent as he presided over the service in the lodge, was quite a contrast to the way he was now, nude in the swimming pool like everyone else, laughing off the lewd comments being shouted at random. Thomas remembered Randy's words from the other day — *it's like he's one of us.*

"I'm Father Stumpf." He held out his hand. He was of medium height and build his body looked soft, although not fat. The light brown hair on his head was receding but the rest of him was covered with it—beast-like.

Thomas took the priest's wet hand in his own and although embarrassed to be standing naked in front of a grown man, a holy man nonetheless, he was glad that Father had sought him out amidst all the noisy fun going on around them.

"Father Henderson tells me you're fifteen. He told me about the boy with the cut on his head. He said you saved the day." He smiled as he spoke, his teeth gleaming in the moonlight.

They've talked about me? Thomas Paul was intoxicated by the fact that they had discussed him in an apparent good light.

Throughout the evening they talked, laughed, splashed, and cavorted in the pool. No one had ever lavished such attention on Thomas. Soon, without realizing it, they were the only two left in the water. Thomas was giddy with nervous excitement as they continued splashing around and rough-housing.

Then, without much thought, he reached over to pick Father Bob up out of the water and toss him back in. In reaching to grab his leg, his hand accidentally landed on the priest's penis. It was fully erect. Embarrassed and blushing, Thomas pretended not to notice what he had done and with a great adrenaline rush, tossed the man across the water. Father Bob, in an honest state of surprise, laughed and marveled as he wiped the water from his eyes. "You're strong like an ox! You're stronger than most men I know."

Thomas tossed the priest again but this time made sure he did not grab him the same way, and before Father Bob could surface, Thomas Paul swam to the ladder and climbed out of the pool. He was reluctant to end their fun but also anxious and confused—unable to forget the priest's obvious arousal.

They made small talk while they toweled off and returned to their respective cabins. Father Bob left camp the next morning, with much less fanfare. He did not return to Evergreen that summer.

Chapter 11

August 15th, 1975

Dear Thomas Paul,

In my many years as director of Camp Evergreen, I have been blessed to know hundreds of boys and young men. Naturally, some have stood out more than others — for both good reasons, and, at times, not-so-good reasons. But, through our Heavenly Father, I have loved and enjoyed each and every one of them!

You are a wonderful young man, and you have many gifts and talents. However, I must admit that I see you are often troubled and distracted. I worry about you and your behavior this past summer. Some counselors have complained that you can be aloof, difficult to be around, and don't always finish your share of the work. I have defended you at every turn and I have encouraged patience and understanding, as I know you are as deserving as all others.

I can see the light inside of you, Tommy, but I fear it is hidden beneath a tough, crusty exterior that you seem to have built around yourself.

Rather than bother your parents with my concerns, I feel that you are old enough and mature enough for me to speak to directly. I enjoy your presence here at Camp Evergreen, you are an asset to our tribe, and I would like you to return to us in the summers for as long as you so desire.

However, I am asking you to spend some time working on your attitude before returning to camp. We can all benefit from introspection and self-awareness, but it is important that you take some serious time to sort through your thoughts and feelings and hopefully return as a more integral part of our brotherhood.

Please know that I am always available to you for guidance if needed. And, of course, you can always turn to Our Lord at any time of the day or night, as He is always there for us.

"Come to me, all you who are weary and burdened, and I will give you rest."

Matthew 11:28

Blessings,

Father Henderson

Chapter 12

The Stantons had just sat down to Saturday night supper when the phone rang. Thomas Paul and his siblings stopped eating and looked at their father. A dinnertime phone call was one of two things: rude or important. Each child offered a silent prayer that it wasn't one of their friends daring to be so inconsiderate at this time of day surely they knew better by now?

With a frown, their father rested his utensils on the edge of his plate and pushed his chair away from the table. He picked up the receiver on the fifth ring.

"Hello," he said, his tone firm but restrained.

The children held their breath as they pushed the food around on their plates, waiting and wondering who was on the other end of the line.

"Yes, Father," he said with surprise, the furrow in his brow smoothing. "No, no. It's not a bad time at all."

All ears at the table perked up. Father who? Who could it be? They looked at each other for clues as they tried to decipher the conversation from the few words out of their father's mouth.

"Is that so? Well, that sounds wonderful. I'm sure he would

like that... Next weekend? Yes, yes, that would be fine ...
Wonderful, we'll be expecting you. Thank you, Father...same to
you."

He replaced the phone in its cradle and returned to the table.

"Who was it Johnny?" their mother asked.

Thomas Paul felt his father's eyes on him. He returned his
gaze and saw a smile on his father's face.

"That was Father Stumpf," he said with pride. "From St.
Bartholomew's parish. Apparently, you met him at camp this
summer?" The question was directed at his younger son. "Seems
you made quite an impression on him." Thomas swallowed and
felt his pulse start to flutter.

His father continued. "He called to invite our younger son
here to his lake house. He and two other priests, another one
from camp, Father Monroe are taking a group of boys for an
overnight stay. They do this every once in a while, apparently."

Every eye at the table widened. The importance of an
invitation like this, from such an esteemed individual — a priest
was not lost on Thomas Paul's parents. Even his mother was
thrilled. They looked at him with pleasant surprise. Their misfit
son, at times so painful to embrace, had been chosen from
dozens of other boys to spend personal time with a man of the
cloth. Any Christian family would have seen it as a wonderful
blessing.

"Lake house? You are so lucky!" his younger sister said.

Thomas Paul couldn't imagine such a thing. Did people
really own lake houses? It was something so far removed from
his own middle-class reality. He might as well have been invited
on a trip to Disneyland.

Thomas Paul thought of nothing else all week. He watched
the seconds, minutes and hours tick by at school and couldn't

wait to get to sleep at night so that another day would pass and he would wake one day closer to Friday.

He wondered about the other boys that would be there, and if any of them would be his friends from camp. He hoped he would fit in. Maybe the personal invitation from Father Bob was all he would need. Perhaps that alone would guarantee the others would like him. To everyone else at camp, Father Bob was beyond cool. Surely being hand-picked by him would count for something.

He raced home from school on Friday, his overnight bag already packed and waiting. Father Bob was to come by the house and pick Thomas up himself. In honor of the priest's visit, Thomas Paul's father had arranged to be home from work early that Friday. Thomas and his mother alternated between pacing and glancing out the window, watching for a vehicle to approach the house.

"Now, son, I know I don't have to tell you to be on your absolute best behavior, do I?" Thomas Paul's father said as his mother peered out the window and down the street.

"No, sir," Thomas replied.

"I know you guys will be goofing off and having fun but you will use your manners and show respect at all times."

"Yes, sir. I will."

Father Bob's car pulled up to the house at 4:00 p.m. sharp. "He's here!" Thomas Paul's mother said. "Do you think he'll come to the door?"

"He goddamn well better come to the door," his father said.

Thomas Paul's father was honored that his son had been selected to go to the lake but at the same time, he felt that his children were certainly as deserving of any others in the archdiocese. He was as devout, church-going, and God-fearing as anyone, but the church had ignited his fury when they turned down his daughter's admission to the parish school. They said the Stantons hadn't tithed enough in years past. As far as he was concerned, they could all go to hell. Fuck the damn church.

He was beneath no one. People drove on his roads, shopped in his stores, went to his church, filled up at his gas station, ate at his restaurants, and lived in his neighborhood. This priest was most certainly going to come to his door and greet his wife and fetch his son.

With a smile upon his face, Thomas Paul's father opened the door before Father even had a chance to knock or ring the bell.

"Come on in, Father Bob," he said, holding out his hand.

"Thank you, John." Father smiled and returned the handshake.

"Heck of a lovely day out there, isn't it?"

"It sure is. A beautiful day."

Thomas Paul stood to the side and watched his father work his magical personality on the priest. He was one of the finest pharmaceutical salesmen in the state and when he was on, it was impossible not to like him. When he wanted to be, he was funny, charming, patient, and well-spoken. He could converse with anyone, from the most educated physicians or reverent priests to the simple store clerk or kind, country neighbor. Thomas Paul and his siblings often wished and prayed that when their father returned home on Fridays, he wouldn't have to leave his work personality at the door.

Father Bob greeted Thomas Paul's mother and shared a few

words with Anne Marie, also home from school to see Thomas off on his adventure. Father wore black pants, a short sleeved, black, button-down shirt, and his white collar. Thomas could sense his father's pride in having such a well-respected person visit his home.

Finally, the priest acknowledged Thomas Paul.

"Well, Thomas, are you ready for a fun night with the gang?" he smiled.

"Yes, Father," he beamed.

Father Bob turned to Thomas Paul's parents once more. "I knew the minute I spotted your son at Camp Evergreen that he was a special young man. Father Henderson also speaks very highly of him."

His parents' faces showed a mixture of pleasure and yet surprise that their son had made such an impression.

"He'll get to meet an exceptional bunch of boys, all students at St. Victor. I and two fellow priests will be chaperoning."

St. Victor's was one of the top all-boys Christian high schools in the city. It was a well-known, deeply traditional brotherhood of students and alumni made up of those fortunate enough to be able to afford it. St. V's! Thomas thought to himself. Almost every young boy in the city dreamed of going to high school at St. Victor's. Again, Thomas Paul hoped these boys would like him.

As Thomas followed Father to the car, he turned and waved to his parents, their pleasure evident on their faces. Finally, he thought to himself, he'd done something good to make them happy.

"Have a good time, son... bye, honey," his parents said, waving goodbye from their front porch.

"So how far is it to the lake?" Thomas asked.

"It's just over an hour." With one hand on the wheel, the priest reached up, unfastened his top shirt button, pulled off his collar and put it on the seat between them.

"What kind of stuff are we gonna do?" Thomas continued.

"Lots of fun things. You know, like at camp. Things boys do together. Swimming, campfires, eating, drinking."

Thomas Paul's mind was jolted back to that night at camp. He thought of the skinny-dipping and horsing around in the pool, alone with Father Bob. His skin prickled with goose bumps.

Father kept talking. "Do you and your friends ever drink, Thomas?"

"Well, I have, once. But isn't that wrong?"

Father Bob laughed. "No, Thomas. Drinking is not wrong. Not if you do it responsibly."

For the rest of the trip, Thomas talked a lot about God. He was very interested in religion and in right and wrong. He wanted to show Father that he was indeed a good Catholic boy, certainly as devout as the boys who went to St. V's. But oddly, Father Bob kept steering the conversation away from all things religious. Maybe he would discuss religion with him later, when all the boys were together.

They pulled up to the house and parked next to several other cars. Nervous but excited, Thomas grabbed his bag and followed the priest inside. The house was rustic, much like a cabin would be. The main floor was a big, open kitchen, an eating area, and a massive great room. The furniture had been rearranged to make room for several sleeping bags strewn in a haphazard circle on the floor. There was also a large wood-burning fireplace with a great stone chimney that ran all the way up the wall.

"Everyone! This is Thomas," Father Bob announced in a voice loud enough to pierce the din of the boisterous group.

Thomas stood behind Father and smiled as all eyes focused on them.

"Hey."

"Hi, Thomas."

"Hey, man!"

They all shouted their hellos and waved back.

"Would you like to be called 'Thomas'?" Father asked.

"Or they can call me Tommy," he answered.

"Our new friend likes to be called Tommy."

"Tommy, that is Father Gus." A middle-aged priest with a dark beard and wire-rimmed glasses waved from behind the kitchen counter.

"Next to him is Father Michael. You remember him from camp?"

"Welcome, Tommy," Father Michael said, smiling. He was obviously the oldest of the three priests and had been a fixture at camp almost as long as Father Henderson. He was chopping vegetables and placing them in a large pot on the gas stove.

Beer was being poured, jokes were being told, and stories

were being shared. It was evident from the stories that some of the boys had been to the lake house before. Thomas wanted to pinch himself. He couldn't believe that he was there, partaking in such camaraderie.

Boys were coming in and out of the house, dripping wet from the lake or sweaty from Frisbee or touch football, eating, drinking, and horsing around without a care in the world. They invited Thomas to join in all their games but still a bit shy, he was content to simply hang back and observe.

Thomas was almost certain he was the youngest boy at the house but, of course, he looked much older than fifteen. There were high-school juniors and seniors and even some college age boys. Thomas looked as old as any of them, even older than some.

He stepped outside and, having seen several other boys smoking, lit a cigarette from a pack he had retrieved from his bag. It was a new habit he had picked up in the last six months. His mother was okay with it and gave him cigarettes every now and then, just another secret they kept from his father.

"You smoke?" Father Bob appeared next to him on the porch.

"Yeah. I'm sorry, am I too young? " Thomas hesitated and was ready to step on the butt and snuff it out.

"No, no, don't worry, Tommy. It's perfectly fine," he said. "I just didn't know you were a smoker."

"So, do you smoke anything else?"

Thomas knew what he meant and was startled by the question but didn't want it to show. "Oh, yeah. Sure! Doesn't everyone?" He lied.

Father smiled again. "Well, maybe I'll have to bring some grass for us to smoke next time you come out to the lake."

Next time? Thomas thought, happily.

"You want a beer? We usually only let the eighteen year olds drink, but you can have one if you want to."

"Nah, I'm okay right now. Thanks, though."

As the evening continued and darkness fell, many in the group were drunk, hooting and hollering, wanting to skinny-dip. Thomas was thankful it was dark. He was so happy to be a part of the gang. They had welcomed him with ease, just like he had hoped and prayed. No doubt his looks had helped, as well. Judging strictly by his physical appearance, he was a very handsome young man — the embodiment of a star athlete or of someone who was surely one of the most popular kids in school.

But Thomas was worried that if he let his guard down and became too comfortable, they would all see what he really was —an anxious, broken, scared little kid who didn't fit in anywhere. Still, for now, he thought only positive thoughts. This was even better than camp.

Finally, after midnight, most of the boys were passed out on or in their sleeping bags. Thomas placed his own sleeping bag in a corner next to one that had not been unrolled, an extra, maybe. Or perhaps one of the boys had claimed the couch instead of joining the others on the floor. Either way, he was happy to have a little extra room.

The priests occupied the bedrooms on the upper level of the house, and Father Bob had not bid them goodnight. No matter, Thomas was happy and tired. He thought about Father Henderson's letter to him at the end of the summer. He wondered if this overnight stay with these new acquaintances could count as a sort of self-analysis. Father Bob surely would report to Father Henderson how well he had gotten along with everyone. Maybe there was hope for him yet.

Just then, he felt a clammy hand on his naked shoulder.

"Tommy, are you comfortable?" Father Bob whispered to him.

"Oh, yes, thanks."

"Are you sure? Because you are more than welcome to come and sleep in my room with me. It's very comfortable. Much better than the floor."

Father's hand did not leave Thomas Paul's shoulder. Thomas was confused. The priest had been so kind to invite him to the lake; would it be rude to decline? But he wanted to stay where he was, with the rest of the guys.

"No, that's okay. I'm really fine right here."

Father Bob hesitated for what seemed like a long time and sighed. "Alright then." He squeezed and patted Thomas Paul's shoulder, then walked away.

Thomas Paul's heart pounded in his chest. It was very dark but in the glow from the light in the kitchen, he had caught something in the priest's eyes. He wasn't quite sure what it was but before long, it was forgotten.

He stayed awake for a while longer, with a smile on his face. Thomas was only fifteen—but fifteen years is a long time to wait to feel accepted, even liked by your peers. He was elated.

Months later, in the dead of winter, Thomas Paul's parents got another phone call. It seemed Father Bob had not forgotten about their son.

Chapter 13

The second trip to the lake house was a departure from the first. Unbeknownst to Thomas Paul's parents, and to Thomas himself, there were no other guests. It was to be a party of two.

It was late winter. There was no snow on the ground, and the days were warm in the sunshine but the nights were cold. Within moments of arriving at the house, Father Bob lead Thomas down to the dock, and they went out on the water in a small, motorized fishing boat. They headed towards the middle of the lake. The air was fresh and the water was clear and still, like glass. After a short while, Father Bob cut the engine and moved aside.

"Your turn," he smiled.

"Really?" Thomas asked.

"Of course. You can do it."

Thomas traded places with the priest, then pulled the cord and started the motor again. He gripped the handle of the motor, just as Father Bob had done, and steered the boat forward. He smiled widely as the small craft cut through the water. It was exhilarating and liberating to be captaining a boat, regardless of the size. Thomas Paul was quite entertained by the experience and could feel the priest watching him.

"Wow, look at you!" Father Bob said. "You're a pro already. I knew you would be."

"You think so?" Thomas smiled.

"Absolutely. Have you done this before?"

Thomas shook his head. "No, never. Well, I mean, I've been on my uncle's fishing boat, when I was little. But I've never actually driven one like this." He felt very grown-up and proud that Father trusted him to be in control of the small vessel.

They spent several hours trolling around on the water, the sky above blue and bright. It was peaceful and glorious. Father Bob did most of the talking while Thomas steered the boat up and down the lake.

The priest had traveled the world and was, by a lifetime, Thomas Paul's emotional, intellectual, and spiritual superior. Through his education and the priesthood, Father Bob had been exposed to an endless universe that Thomas Paul couldn't even fathom. Thomas was dumbfounded that this man wanted to spend time with him.

They returned to the dock late in the afternoon and walked back to the house side by side. Father Bob put his arm around Thomas Paul.

"You know, Tommy, you remind me of myself at your age."

Thomas Paul's eyes widened. "Really? I do?"

The priest laughed. "I wasn't blessed with your looks but in other ways, yes, for sure."

Thomas was speechless. He couldn't imagine that this man had ever felt the things Thomas felt now. He couldn't believe that the priest had ever been disliked, insecure, tortured or picked on.

Thomas set the table while Father cooked an Italian dinner of salad and pasta, following recipes he had learned while studying in Rome. He drank red wine while he cooked. Thomas accepted a glass, after the priest assured him it wasn't a sin to do so, but didn't want to admit he hated the taste of it.

As they sat down to eat, Thomas waited for the priest to say grace over the steaming, fragrant meal. But Father Bob stabbed his fork into his salad almost immediately.

"Shouldn't we pray before we eat?" Thomas asked.

Father half-smiled and shook his head as he chewed. "Sometimes it's fine to just say it to yourself. Dig in."

Thomas shrugged and started eating. He had never tasted anything so good. It was like dining in a restaurant.

"So, did you always want to be a priest when you were a kid?" Thomas asked.

"Not really."

"When did you know you wanted to become one?" he continued.

"Oh, I don't know. When I was about your age, maybe."

"Really?"

"What about you, Tommy? What do you want to be when you grow up?"

Thomas ignored the question. He felt confident around Father Bob and wanted to appear grown-up around him. He wanted to impress him with what little knowledge he possessed and religion was one area where he felt he had a thing or two to share. "You know, I've been saved. I have a good friend, Sadie. She's a Christian. A true Christian. We read the Bible together a lot and."

Father cut him off. "Tommy, first of all, you shouldn't be reading the Bible without a priest. A priest will help you interpret the teachings of the Bible. It is far too complex to do alone. Secondly, this friend of yours, she's an Evangelical I presume?"

Thomas nodded.

"Look, the name *Christian* predates the Evangelical community by over a millennium, as does the word *Bible*. Any organization that says Catholics are not Christians is seriously misguided because they are ignoring the history of Christianity.

The Catholic Church chose which books to include in the Bible. Catholics protected the Bible through centuries of wars, famines, plagues, the fall of Rome, fires, and threats from all sides. This was long before any other denomination existed. And the Catholic Church protected Christianity from Arian heresy that almost gutted Christianity in the 4th century. He took a sip of wine. "I could go on for a long time but the purpose of this weekend was not to give you a religion lesson. I don't know your friend, but maybe you two should talk about other things once in a while and save the Bible study for church."

Thomas nodded in silence. His mouth was dry all of sudden but he had no desire for anymore wine.

"Now, where were we?" Father smiled. "What do you think about doing when you finish school?"

"I haven't really thought about it," Thomas said as he reached for his water glass. "I like art. I'm a pretty good drawer."

"I'm not surprised. I bet you're good at everything you do."

Thomas felt himself blush. The dinner conversation continued. They laughed and joked with each other and despite Thomas Paul's earlier gaffe at attempting to educate the priest about being saved, he felt at ease. He'd never felt this sure of himself in front of an adult before. Father Bob seemed genuinely interested in what he had to say.

In truth, Thomas Paul was slowly developing into a bright, brave, and assured human being. Deep down inside, at the core, a friendly, confident, enthusiastic young man was waiting to emerge—like tonight. But time after time someone would stomp that promising young man back down into oblivion, often for nothing more than the feelings his looks and mannerisms provoked in others. Maybe Father Bob would be the mentor he needed to nurture that lost soul before it was too late.

After the dishes were dried and put away, they retreated to the great room.

"Have you actually grown in the few months since we were last here? I can't believe you might be even stronger than that night you tossed me across the pool at camp!" the priest said laughing.

Thomas smiled. "I don't think so."

"Well, you might be strong in the water but I bet I might be stronger on land." He laughed some more as he jabbed Thomas in the ribs, then wrapped his arms around him and gently pushed him to the floor.

Thomas did not doubt his strength but he doubted his talent at wrestling, which was basically another sport. When he was smaller, his brother had tormented him constantly, tackling him to the ground until he gave up—which was always quickly. This was different.

They rolled around and tussled with each other yet it was not mean or forceful but, rather, playful and encouraging. The priest seemed to be out of breath although they were hardly exerting themselves. All of a sudden, Thomas found himself flat on his back, and Father Bob rolled on top of him. But, rather than drawing up his knees and straddling him while pinning his arms at his sides, like his brother had always done, the priest lay down with his whole body pressed on top of him and placed his head next to Thomas Paul's so that they were cheek to cheek. Thomas lay there motionless, with his eyes wide open, and once again felt the priest's hardness. Only this time, it was pressing firmly against him. His breath was heavy in Thomas Paul's ear. It reminded him of the way Sally used to breathe when they would roll around on the couch in her basement.

After only a second, Father pulled himself up and laughed. "I won!"

The night had become cold, and Father Bob built a large crackling fire in the hearth. Thomas had never even been in front of a fireplace before except during his first visit to the cabin months before. During the summer it hadn't been lit—but now in the winter, he was mesmerized by the bright, flickering flames.

Father excused himself for a moment and returned carrying a small plastic baggie.

"You like to smoke pot, right?"

Thomas remembered the conversation from their last trip. "Oh, yeah, for sure. But it doesn't really do anything to me." He lied, repeating something he had heard someone say. "So, priests can smoke pot?" he asked as he watched Father roll the dried plant in a thin white rolling paper.

Father Bob sighed. "Tommy, priests are human. We can do a lot of things that everyone else does. What people do when they're together, in private, is their own business. That goes for you, me, and everyone else, including the Pope." He licked the thin line of glue on the paper, pressed the seam and sealed it, rolled the wrinkly cigarette back and forth in his fingers a few times, then flicked a lighter that he also carried in the small bag, and lit the joint.

Thomas watched the priest inhale the pungent smoke into his lungs. He was thankful that he did at least smoke regular cigarettes so he wouldn't look like a total amateur when Father passed the joint to him.

In no time, they were both flying high. Thomas was awash in warmth and peaceful happiness. It was the most wonderful thing he had ever felt. They talked and giggled about everything and nothing. After what seemed like hours of pure bliss, Thomas felt himself drifting off. The roaring fire had turned to warm red and grey embers. Father Bob nudged Thomas, rose to his feet and suggested that it was time for bed.

"When nobody is here in the winter, we keep the unused bedrooms closed off from the heating system. Would you mind sleeping in my room with me?" he said.

"No, I don't mind," Thomas answered.

He followed Father Bob into the bedroom and noticed there was only one bed. Despite his senses being dulled by the pot, a subtle feeling of anxiety came over him. Nonetheless, he watched the priest undress down to his underwear and climb into bed, and followed suit without a word. The flannel sheets were cool and inviting. He was drowsy and asleep within moments.

In the darkness, as the fog from his marijuana-induced sleep lifted, Thomas Paul found himself awake, lying on his side. He became aware that Father Bob was pressed up against him. Thomas did not move and waited, wondering if the priest was asleep. A short moment later, he felt the man's arm wrap around him and pull him even closer.

Thomas Paul's heart exploded in his chest. There was no mistaking what the priest was doing. Thomas was paralyzed with fear. The priest, assuming that Thomas Paul's paralysis offered his silent consent, pulled the boy over onto his back and then, just as he had done earlier in the wrestling match, positioned himself on top of him.

Thomas remembered the sight and the touch of the priest's soft, hairy, wet body from the skinny-dipping incident at camp. But this was very different. The sensation of his body being pressed so closely against his own filled him with something he could not describe. Father Bob released his full weight onto Thomas Paul and pushed his stone-hard penis against the boy's groin until he felt him become aroused. They were both silent, and although Thomas Paul's heart still pounded in his chest, he was barely breathing. The priest waited for a moment, one last time, for an objection or some sort of reaction, but Thomas remained paralyzed. With slow, deliberate movements, the priest gyrated his pelvis for several moments.

In a swift motion, he pulled down his own underwear and then Thomas Paul's. Again, he lowered his fleshy, bestial body down onto Thomas and hunched the boy, harder and faster— then ejaculated. The priest immediately rolled over and pulled Thomas on top of him. He grabbed the boy's hips and pushed and pulled him up and down until he, once more, and Thomas Paul, ejaculated.

Thomas rolled onto his back, speechless.

The priest got up from the bed. "I'll get a warm washcloth."

Thomas Paul was catatonic. He was horrified over what had just happened and remained awake for the rest of the night, staring into the darkness, counting the minutes until dawn.

After several futile attempts by the priest to make conversation, they carried out the next morning's tasks in complete silence. Thomas Paul could not, would not, speak a word. Neither one of them uttered a sound on the trip home.

They pulled up to the house, and Thomas grabbed his overnight bag. As he reached for the door handle, Father Bob spoke one last time.

"It was real."

Thomas said nothing as he walked away.

He didn't, couldn't, know that he had been chosen and preyed upon, groomed, since the very first sunny day at camp when the priest had spotted him, glistening by the pool. It would take years until he understood the intricate steps taken by the priest to perfect the damaging seduction. What he also didn't know was that after this night, although his mind and his heart remained unchanged, his sexual feelings towards girls would never, ever, be the same again.

The only thing Thomas Paul knew, without a shadow of a doubt, was that he had committed a horrible sin.

Chapter 14

Thomas Paul felt an overwhelming sense of impending doom upon returning from the lake. The burning guilt of what he had done coursed through his veins as if it had been injected directly into his body. *This is surely how a murderer must feel,* he thought to himself. A man lying with another man. It was even more abominable than simple fornication. The Bible said it and therefore there was no questioning it — he was morbid.

After school on Monday, Thomas, in a panic, hurried to seek refuge at the only place he knew — he would confess his sins to Sadie. She would pray over him and he would find absolution. He knocked on the door and waited.

"Well, hello there, stranger!" Sadie smiled. "We haven't seen you all weekend." Her smile faded as soon as she noticed the obvious look of torment on Thomas Paul's face.

"What's the matter, Tommy? You don't look well."

"I'm not," Thomas said. Tears welled in his eyes as he stepped into the house.

Sadie ushered him over to the table, where they often sat together and prayed. Thomas felt a sense of ease just being there with her.

"Tell me what's on your mind. We'll pray about it and give it up to the Lord. Jesus lifts all our burdens. All we have to do is ask." She smiled and patted his hand.

Thomas did not hesitate. "I did something really bad Sadie, and I don't know what to do about it." His tears lead to sobs as he spoke.

"If you want to tell me what it is, you can. But Jesus has already forgiven you. Looks like you're gonna be the one hardest on yourself." She offered a comforting smile.

Thomas looked her straight in the eye. "I...committed fornication."

Sadie was silent and her face grew dark. She pushed herself away from the table, walked over to the sink and started washing a pile of dirty dishes. She vigorously scrubbed and splashed, clinking and clanging the plates, pots and pans. Thomas flinched, unnerved by the noisemaking—a harsh contrast to Sadie's deafening silence. He waited and tried to stop his tears from falling. He was shocked and confused by Sadie's behavior and sudden coolness towards him. Without turning to look at him, she finally spoke. "That's a really bad sin Thomas. The Bible says Jesus forgives all sins, but I think you should go home and pray a long time about this one to show that you are truly repentant."

She stopped washing but still did not turn to face him. "I have to be able to forgive you, too, so it will be best if you don't come back for a while." The disappointment and sadness in her voice were evident. For a moment, Thomas felt worse about Sadie's feelings towards him than the Lord's. He was silent. The veins in his temples began to pound and throb. His despair, now unbearable, combined with his confusion at her reaction to his confession, made him nauseous.

At last, she faced him. "Go on and walk home now, before it gets dark, so you won't be afraid. I'll let you know when it's okay to come back."

Speechless, Thomas Paul got up from the table and left the house, crying all the way home.

The next day after school, tired from fitful sleep, Thomas walked into the house and was engulfed in the ever-present, oppressive cloud of gloom that permeated the house when his father was on the road. The place was already a pigsty, and he'd only been gone for two days.

"Hello?" he called out.

Silence.

He did not want to be there, but there was nowhere else to go and nobody to turn to. Sadie casting him aside was the final blow to his crumbling dignity. For years now, he had walked the halls of school in fear, but now his fear was almost surpassed by his deep shame. He was disliked by many of his peers, but he never really knew the reason. Now, he was certain that anybody who looked at him would know what he had done. It might as well have been tattooed on his forehead.

Thomas Paul was a shell of a person; friendless, without a shred of confidence, afraid to even look others in the eye anymore. It was no wonder that people avoided him quite simply, he was uncomfortable to be around. He retreated deeper into himself than ever before.

He felt the walls of the house closing in around him—his head throbbed. He wanted to die. He wasn't really scared to die it sounded like sweet relief to him. And he wasn't worried about the pain and sorrow that taking his life would inflict on his family. In all honesty, he didn't feel like anyone would really miss him. The only thing stopping him was the memory of his already failed attempt the year before.

Obviously, God wanted him alive or he would surely have died from the overdose of pills. To attempt to take his own life again, when the Lord had already clearly saved him once, would be the ultimate sin. Worse than the one he had just committed. Suicide was not the answer.

Unable to think of any other escape, he decided to run away.

Thomas Paul set out on foot with nothing but the clothes on his back and no idea where he would go. Before long, without thinking, he felt himself heading in the direction of the church, several miles away, where he had been saved with Sadie and her family. Sadie had failed to ease his guilt and perhaps had even added to it. Thomas felt that the church and Jesus himself surely would.

They had to.

The doors to the church were open and the place was deserted. Thomas Paul felt a familiar peace come over him upon entering. He went to the small, side chapel, walked up to the altar and lay face down, prostrate, with his hands stretched out beside him like Jesus on the cross, in complete submission to his Creator. He began to pray.

Seized by emotional pandemonium, he began to speak in tongues, just as he had a year before when he 'fell out into the spirit' for the first time. That day, everyone around him had complimented him afterwards on how beautiful it was to listen to his 'tongue'. Now, again, he spouted the same fluid vocalizing of speech-like syllables and soon entered a meditative state of mind.

It wasn't long before his guilt began to ease and he felt forgiveness in his heart. God was answering his prayers. He would now be able to hide his sin from everyone. His family members had been drilling him since returning from the lake. They wondered why he was so depressed. He would never tell anyone else what he had done.

Hours later, Thomas pushed himself up off the floor of the church and started the long walk home. He hoped no one would see him. What if his mother happened to drive by and ask why he was walking so far from their house? He hurried home, happy that his headache was gone and that his heart felt lighter.

Thomas Paul turned sixteen but skipped camp that summer. Although his remorse had been somewhat assuaged by literally throwing himself down before God, confessing his sin and praying for absolution, he wasn't about to risk running into Father Bob.

School started again in the fall and Thomas went about his days as usual—trying not to make any waves. He had started to spend more time at church than ever before. He already went with his father and siblings every Sunday without fail. But now that he had his driver's license, he took the car and without anyone knowing, went several times a week. He would go after school or after supper, depending on when the service was at the church of his choosing.

His constant presence at church impressed Sadie and led her to welcome him back into her life and home. It was the only place where he could escape the torment of his everyday life and find some sort of peace.

Still, something had changed. Something had been fully awakened inside of him—a sexual tension over which he was powerless. More than ever, he found himself terrified of boys and the feelings they evoked in him. He was a confused, hormone-fueled sixteen-year-old, aroused at the drop of a hat, with no outlet for his physical desires.

One day in early fall, full of self-loathing, he found himself in his basement with the phone in his hand, calling the only other person in the world he was certain wouldn't turn him away. He sat for a long time, listening to the dial tone hum in his ear. Finally, with reluctance, his hand sweaty and trembling, he dialed the faded number he had scratched onto a scrap of paper.

The phone rang several times in his ear. He prayed nobody would pick up on the other end. He made himself a silent promise that if his call wasn't answered, it was a sign that he should not be doing this, and he would not attempt a second try. Just as he was about to hang up, the priest answered.

"Hello."

"Father Bob? It's Thomas Stanton," he whispered, his voice laden with anxiety.

"Well, hello, Tommy," he said, then hesitated for a split second. "How have you been?"

Thomas could hear the smile in the priest's voice. "I'm okay," he answered.

"How's school going this year?"

"It's fine."

"Good to hear. You know, I was just thinking about you the other day. Do you have any plans for Labor Day?"

"No, I don't think so," Thomas answered.

"Well, how about coming with me to a barbecue. It'll be a great time, at the home of some friends of mine."

"Okay...sure."

It turned out to be a fun, festive get-together at a grand home in a neighborhood Thomas had never been to before. He was in awe of the house: its size, its décor, its furnishings—he had never been inside such a home. Again there was alcohol, food and pot readily available to everyone and as Father Bob wandered around introducing with pride his new friend, Tommy, it was obvious to Thomas Paul that the priest was well liked by all. People clamored to get around Father Bob and spend time talking and joking with him.

"Who's this handsome young man with you, Father Bob?" someone asked.

"This is Tommy Stanton. He's a good friend of mine."

Thomas nodded and smiled at the small group surrounding them

"Are you at St. V's, Tommy?" a woman asked. She was dressed to the nines and wore gold and diamond jewelry on almost every piece of her exposed skin. Thomas had never seen so much jewelry on one woman, and he marveled how dressed up she was for a backyard barbecue.

The priest answered for him. "I haven't been able to convert him yet. But he'd be a great asset to the school."

The woman smiled. Her teeth were pearly white but smudged with bright pink lipstick. "Maybe next year, then. I would love to see you on campus." She winked and sipped her drink. "Honey, you are the most handsome young man I have ever laid eyes on. You must drive the girls wild with those pretty blue eyes!"

"Thank you, ma'am." Thomas felt himself blush.

"Careful, Ray!" Father Bob laughed and addressed the woman's husband. "Barb's at it again. You better keep an eye on her."

The husband guffawed. "Damn it, I thought I cut her off. She was drinking water a minute ago. Somebody must have turned it into wine again!"

The crowd chuckled, hooted and hollered. The atmosphere was even more casual than at the lake however this time there were only adults present. Thomas was clearly the youngest one there and felt very grown-up to be welcomed at such a party. He didn't mind what people thought about his relationship with the priest. If nobody else worried about it, then for one night, he wouldn't either. He pushed everything to the back of his mind and just enjoyed himself, basking in the attention lavished upon him.

A few weeks later, Thomas dialed the priest's phone number again.

"Hello?"

"Father Bob?"

"Yes, Tommy. Great to hear from you again."

"Thanks again for taking me to that party."

"I'm glad you enjoyed yourself. I received a lot of compliments about you."

"Really?"

"Yes. Surely you're not surprised?"

Thomas Paul was caught off guard by the comment and remained silent.

"So, what are you up to this weekend?"

"Not much."

"Well, why don't you come by the rectory? I'll fix you dinner."

"But...don't you live there with other priests?"

"Yeah, it's fine though. We have people over all the time."

"Well ... okay."

The next evening, fidgeting with the car keys in his hand, Thomas stood before his father. His heart pounded in his chest.

"Good!" his father said. "We hadn't heard you mention Father in a long time. We're glad you're going over to spend time with him again. Be careful with the car." He returned his gaze to his newspaper.

"Yes, sir." Thomas Paul's mouth was dry.

As he shut the car door, he also shut down his mind as best he could and drove, in denial, to the home shared by Father Bob and two other priests. The house was surrounded by trees and nestled in the suburbs of a middle-class neighborhood, directly next to the church.

Thomas peeked inside the screen door as he rang the bell and saw a figure wave him in.

"Come on in, Tommy," Father Bob called out.

"Okay."

Thomas wiped his feet and walked towards the voice. He could smell food cooking and his mouth watered. His eyes widened when he reached the kitchen and saw Father Bob standing at the sink with his shirt off. The priest dried his hands on a dishtowel and smiled.

"You're right on time. I'm glad you found the house."

"Yeah, it was no problem," Thomas said.

"Well, have a seat and take it easy. Dinner is just about ready."

Father busied himself at the counter again, chopping and stirring and checking in the oven. Thomas couldn't help but study and stare at the priest's naked torso. He hadn't changed from what Thomas could remember. He wasn't large and he wasn't small. He had an average build, with no muscular definition. The ever-present hair covered every inch of him except on his balding head and where the barber obviously shaved his neck to right above where his shirt collar would reach. Thomas could see lines and folds on the priest's neck. He looked older than his twenty-eight years.

Thomas Paul set the table while Father Bob finished preparing the meal. Then the priest put his shirt back on and they sat down to eat. No one else joined them even though Thomas had seen another car in the driveway and could hear a muffled male voice in another room.

Father Bob made meatloaf and mashed potatoes. It was tasty and hearty, and Thomas ate two helpings. The priest sat back in his chair and enjoyed a glass of red wine while taking pleasure in watching Thomas clear his plate.

"Would you like some wine?" he offered.

"No, thank you. Water is fine."

When the dishes were done, without a word, he followed Father Bob back to his bedroom.

The room was large and furnished like a suite. A bed, sofa, armchair, television, some lamps, and a few small tables were positioned so that they made a sleeping area and a separate sitting area. The priest turned two lamps on and flipped off the ceiling light. Thomas turned on the TV, then flopped down on the couch. Father Bob went directly to his bedside table, opened the top drawer, and then joined Thomas on the couch, a small tin box in hand. Curious, Thomas watched the priest flip open the lid of the box. Inside, a small bunch of joints were bundled together next to a pack of matches.

After only a few draws on the joint, Thomas was high and smiled as he leaned his head back against the couch. It felt even better than the first time at the lake, if that were possible. Thomas never felt this euphoric, relaxed, and carefree on his own. He looked around the room and smiled. Being with Father Bob was cool—it was that simple. He felt comfortable there and at the same time, though he didn't know the word for it, he felt titillated.

Before long, they were laughing and horsing around, just as they had at the lake house. Then, without hesitation, knowing that he was now in full control, as he had long ago planned for this moment, Father Bob started to massage Thomas. Soon, the priest, breathing heavily, took off his clothes and Thomas followed suit. In a whirlwind of grabbing and groping, the priest lay down on his stomach and pulled the boy down on top of him. Thomas Paul's heart raced and his stomach tightened, his mind filled with contradiction.

"Hold on a second," the priest whispered. "Let me get some lubrication."

Thomas laid completely still, his breath caught in his throat, while Father Bob went to his bedside drawer again, retrieved a small bottle of baby oil, and returned to the couch. He flipped open the cap, squirted some of the clear fluid into his palm and lubricated them both, then positioned himself for the boy to enter him. Although Thomas had never fully understood the concept of anal sex, he knew what the priest wanted from him.

Thomas braced himself, with one arm on the back of the sofa and the other on the seat, trying not to touch any part of the man's body. Sensing that Thomas was confused about how to proceed, the priest reached around and guided Thomas inside of him.

It felt foreign and repugnant to be doing such a thing. He was repulsed by the squishy feeling and did not want to continue. The priest moaned in pain and in seconds, as he realized he could not endure the sodomy, he sensed that Thomas was recoiling from the act as well.

Before Thomas could react, the priest quickly turned over onto his back, pulled Thomas down on top of him, and repeated what he had done to him at the lake house.

"Let me go get a towel," the priest said in a sensual tone.

Father Bob pulled on his pants and went out into the hallway, returning moments later with a warm, wet towel, and handed it to Thomas Paul.

In silence, Thomas wiped himself off and put his clothes back on.

"What time do you have to be home? Are your parents expecting you soon?" Father Bob asked.

"Yes, I need to go." *I want to leave and never come back here again.*

Thomas Paul's mind raced. He wanted to run so far away from this place, and yet part of him didn't want to leave. He hated and resented the priest and yet wanted his approval. He knew in his heart that he liked guys and wanted to be loved by a guy, a peer, someone like Tony White. But in Thomas Paul's desperate, damaged mind, the priest was the closest thing he had to a friend and the only person to whom he could turn. *Go away. I hate you. Come here. I need you. Go away. You repulse me. Come here. Don't abandon me, I have nobody else.*

Thomas Paul despised what he was doing but he couldn't help himself; there was no alternative. Again, his body betrayed his heart and his conscience.

I am the only gay boy in the world and I have nowhere else to go.

"Well, let's get together again sometime."

Thomas nodded and fished the car keys out of his jacket pocket.

"Goodnight, drive safely, Tommy."

"Thanks for dinner." As Thomas stepped out into the hallway, he noticed the light was on in the next room. Startled, he met the eyes of another priest, who was sitting behind a desk. He was older, white-haired, and wrinkled—one of the priests from the lake house. Eyebrows raised over the rim of his glasses, the priest studied Thomas Paul, who was frozen on the spot.

Thomas could not read the man's face or decipher the look he was being given and made his way towards the door as quickly as he could.

He swallowed the small lump in his throat and left the house, closing the door behind him without making any sound.

He drove home in as much denial as when he had arrived.

Chapter 15

Thomas stood in the shower with his head tilted up and his mouth wide open. The water, as hot as he could stand it, filled his mouth and ran down his tongue and off his chin. Repeatedly he swished, gargled, and spat down the drain. The bitterness of the priest's vile semen was finally no longer on his taste buds, but he could not wash the filth that he felt off his body and from his mind, no matter how hard he scrubbed.

This third encounter had been mostly a repeat performance of their previous engagements. A phone call, dinner, compliments, friendly conversation, smoking pot, followed by casual wrestling, the removal of clothing, and silent positioning. Only this time the priest maneuvered Thomas onto his back and then turned his own body around until their faces were in each other's groins.

Without hesitating and despite Thomas Paul's shy attempt to turn his head away, Father Bob pushed his penis into the boy's mouth. Thomas Paul could feel his stomach tighten and begin to churn at the taste and smell of the priest's hairy genitalia.

A morbid obsession was now forming in his psyche. He was horrified and powerless—helpless to stop the damaging injustice being imposed upon him.

The priest bore down forcefully—ejaculating into the boy's mouth after three short thrusts. Thomas Paul could hold back no longer. He choked and gagged violently.

In a state of shock, he pushed himself off the couch, ran to the garbage can next to the priest's bed, and expelled every trace of fluid from his mouth as if it were poison. Within minutes and without words, he was clothed and back in his father's car, speeding away.

What have I done? What have I done? What have I done?

The water in the shower was turning cool. *I'm filth*, Thomas thought to himself, mortified.

It wasn't a conscious decision, but it would be the last time Thomas Paul would ever visit Father Bob. He would return to camp the following summer, at seventeen, and would see the priest, though they would not speak. With unabashed audacity, the priest paraded someone new around the camp.

He was the physical opposite of Thomas in every way and seemed shabby and rough, neglected, even missing a tooth. *My replacement*, Thomas thought to himself. Even though Father Bob and Thomas Paul did not exchange actual words, their eyes met and the priest had plenty to say with his silent stare and facial expression: *I have done nothing wrong and I will not be shamed. You came to me willingly, of your own volition. What we had was mutual and consensual. It's your loss that I have taken someone new.*

The priest was bold but kept his distance, as did most everyone else by now. It had started developing around him as a young boy, in a makeshift teepee in his old neighborhood. Too much had happened to him in his short life and without even being aware of it, Thomas wore an invisible, hard, crusty armor—just like Father Henderson had spoken of in his letter years before. To all who looked at him it said: *Stay away from me. Do not approach.* Built by his subconscious, this shell kept him safe from predators but made him repellent to others—even kind people with good intentions, which his conscious being desperately needed.

The last two years of high school were bearable. He was now physically full-grown, six feet tall, and muscular—his size intimidating. Most of the bullying and torment had ended but still, when he stepped out of his house or into the street, his heart would race, and he awaited it with a familiar, gnawing pain in his gut. He was so conditioned to the mere sight of himself igniting hostile reactions in others that he was unable to let his guard down and rarely felt at ease. Nonetheless, people didn't try to harass him anymore, and despite his coarse demeanor, he even managed to make and keep a few close friends.

Thomas Paul graduated high school with very little fanfare and got a job digging trees in a nursery. He didn't fit in very well with his fellow employees, and his boss despised him. After six months, he was called into the office.

"Stanton, you ain't cut out for this job. Get your things together and go on home now—and don't worry none 'bout comin' back … ya hear?"

Thomas shrugged. "That's okay with me because I've decided I'm going to hair school." He grabbed his last paycheck and walked out the door.

He had no money to pay for an education, but he would find a way to make it happen. He was sure of it.

CHAPTER 16

1978

Thomas took a deep breath and with a clammy hand pulled open the front door of The Hair Design Academy. *Here goes.* Overcoming his shyness and self-doubt, for even a moment, was a huge step for him. He dug deep inside himself for the courage to forge his future. It was the boldest thing he had ever done. He was nervous as he approached the front desk. The receptionist looked up from filing her nails and smiled.

"Well, hello there, blue eyes. How can I help you?" she asked as she chewed her gum.

"I'm interested in going to school here and wondered how to go about it."

Her eyes lit up, obviously pleased at the thought of possibly getting better acquainted with the young, handsome stranger.

"That's great. Have a seat, and I'll see if Miss Sherry's free. She'll be able to tell you more about the program."

She disappeared into the hallway.

Thomas sat down in the row of chairs by the door and picked up a hair-styling magazine. He flipped through the pages of glamorous hairstyles and was inspired at the thought of someday being able to create such beauty with his own hands. He had taught himself to cut hair as a teenager, starting with his own, because his father refused to pay for haircuts from a proper stylist. After butchering it over and over, his technique gradually improved. Impressed with the results of his own lustrous locks, his neighborhood girlfriends would request his services and were quite pleased, as well.

By the time he was eighteen, he could give a well-executed, basic haircut to a guy or a girl. He was sure he could one day be successful and get paid to do the very same thing.

The receptionist returned a moment later, trailing behind a beautiful but older woman who Thomas assumed must be Miss Sherry. She was blonde and voluptuous; her large breasts heaved high on her chest. Her makeup and hair were impeccable and Thomas felt his pulse quicken looking at her.

"Welcome to the Hair Design Academy. I'm Sherry Davis, the manager and head instructor." She offered Thomas a manicured hand, which he accepted. Her nails were very long and painted bright crimson.

"I'm Thomas Paul Stanton."

"We're so happy to have you, Thomas." Sherry stared deep into Thomas Paul's eyes as she spoke.

Happy was an understatement. Thomas reveled in the new attention he was attracting. He was surrounded by adults who, unlike his peers at school, treated him like he was just a regular guy. They saw past his looks and seemed to genuinely like who he was. For the first time since summer camp as a kid, he flourished.

Thomas Paul's father made too much money to qualify for financial aid to help pay for his son's tuition. To add insult to injury, he refused to contribute a single dollar to Thomas' education.

"Son, nobody gave me a goddamn thing since the day I turned eighteen and by God, it made me the man I am today. You want something, you go out and get it yourself, just like I did."

Fortunately, the school administrators were impressed with Thomas Paul's talent and, aware of his dilemma, they approached him with a partial scholarship. At the end of his freshman class, there was a school-wide hair competition that he entered on a whim, knowing he would be competing against seniors who were ready to graduate.

Miss Sherry took it upon herself to coach him and help him prepare. The day of the competition, all students entered in the contest had a limited time frame to do their sets, followed by another timeframe to do comb-outs. When the bell went off, the stylists were required to put down their brushes and were ushered into a private room. The models, wearing numbers to maintain the stylists' anonymity, remained. The judges, waiting in a separate room, were brought in. The hairstyles were then graded on uniqueness and execution.

The judges made their rounds, took notes, and cast their ballots. The stylists were asked for a volunteer to help count the votes and when no hands were raised, Thomas volunteered.

After all the votes were tallied and the winner was determined, the director of the school asked, "Does anybody remember who styled model number thirteen?"

Thomas Paul beamed. After a moment, no longer able to hold back his excitement, he nodded his head and replied. "Yes. It was me."

The following year, Thomas Paul was due to start his clinicals, but he was worried. He still had no money and no idea how he would pay his tuition. One day after class, to his surprise and delight, he was once again approached by the director.

"I have some good news for you. After careful consideration, we have agreed that your talent merits a full scholarship. Congratulations, you will now be able to finish the program."

He was relieved and overjoyed. He wouldn't have to worry about money anymore. There was no going back now.

"You're very talented, Thomas," Sherry said. She stood next to him as he rinsed out the shampoo sink. "You remind me of myself; your technique and dedication — you've certainly paid attention in class."

Thomas could smell her perfume and felt her breasts brush up against his arm as she walked away. *Her breasts.* He looked at them all the time and didn't care that she often caught him staring. Maybe she even enjoyed it. In truth, they stared at each other whenever they were in the same room. Something had come over Thomas Paul when he met Sherry; he had the brazen confidence of a much older, much different man. It was almost as if he wasn't himself. He wanted to seduce her and could sense that she was torn by the feelings he evoked in her. It pleased him to know that he could make her blush and stammer in mid-sentence. He was the only guy surrounded by a sea of women.

Guys, thankfully, had temporarily been pushed to the farthest reach of his mind. Sherry was the only person he wanted to be with.

She was twenty-eight years old and married to a burly, dark-haired man named Jeff, who spent a lot of time at the school. He was funny and friendly, and they both took a liking to Thomas Paul. They often invited him over for dinner. They smoked pot together, something Thomas was very familiar with. To him, it was the one and only thing he had gained from the priest—a love of marijuana. He smoked pot and cigarettes every day—from dawn until dusk.

It was soon known around school that Thomas Paul had become a teacher's pet. His looks and his talent were irresistible to Sherry, and she made no bones about letting him know it.

"You're so good-looking, Thomas. You're pretty, like a girl. Those blue eyes and that golden hair." It was something he heard many times before.

Sherry fawned over him, and he relished the attention. He delighted in her infatuation. It was a dance they did together, in secret, for a long time.

Soon enough, they were meeting alone for make-out sessions in her car or at his brother's house, which just happened to be down the street from the school. In no time, they were ready for their relationship to develop into a full-blown affair and Thomas found himself in love with her. They decided to go away together for a weekend.

"I know a place we can go," Thomas said. "It's a park I used to go to as a kid. I had a lot of good times there and I'd like to show it to you."

"Sounds wonderful. I told Jeff we were going to a hair show."

Of course there was no hair show. They spent the weekend holed up in a rented cabin at Beaver Creek Park. Thomas had the body and desires of a man but still held some of the confusion and clumsiness of an inexperienced teenager, at least where women were concerned. Sherry was eager with arousal for Thomas and would not be sidetracked by his sexual naiveté.

"Push, Thomas…just *push*," she whispered, encouraging him to enter her.

He did as she asked and she cried out, her whole body trembling beneath him. *She must be having an orgasm*, he thought to himself. He was proud that he had pleased her but tried to ignore the fact that he hadn't climaxed himself, praying that she wouldn't mention it.

The sex between them was tender. He was happy and wanted to be with her, but he was in denial about why he had not experienced an orgasm. Thankfully, Sherry, possibly in denial herself, never mentioned it.

They slept intertwined, blissful and spent. Upon returning to the city, Thomas bragged to a fellow student about the affair, which spread through the school like wildfire.

In a matter of days, Jeff, now aware of the situation, went looking for Thomas Paul in a furious, jealous rage. He drove straight to where he knew he would find him—at his brother's house. He bolted up to the porch and rang the doorbell. Thomas opened the door and was greeted by a punch square to his head, breaking Jeff's hand and leaving Thomas stunned.

In a whirlwind of drama the affair was over, and Thomas was informed by the head of the school that he was to be transferred to another branch of The Hair Design Academy. He soldiered on, graduated at the top of his class, and was offered his first job. He was an old hand at chaos, and it would not derail him on his quest for a happy, fulfilled life.

Chapter 17

1982

Thomas found himself almost in a trance as he looked into the piercing blue eyes staring back at him. He now understood what people felt when they looked into his own and why they couldn't resist commenting on them. Renee Keller's eyes were a deep azure blue. They sparkled with happiness and warmth. She was also blond, and Thomas felt an almost immediate kinship with her, like they could have been brother and sister. He felt at home, like he belonged.

"So, Thomas, you're interested in doing some modeling? How did you hear about us?" Renee asked.

"I have a friend who took some classes here and, well, my boss told me that I need to work on my personality, that I am too shy and introverted. I thought this might help me come out of my shell."

"Modeling can be a very fulfilling experience. I think you may have made the right choice. I'm quite sure you've been told before that you're a very good-looking guy?" Renee smiled.

Thomas felt himself blush. "I suppose so."

"You have a great look, but do you think you might be willing to cut your hair?"

Thomas beamed at the reality that Renee actually seemed to be welcoming him to Click, the hottest agency in the city. "I am willing to do anything you recommend. I love it here already and completely trust you."

"That is a refreshing attitude and just what you will need in this industry if you want to be successful," Renee said.

He would soon undergo a complete external transformation. The modeling classes and the people at Click would help him shed his out-of-style, pedestrian look— starting with his long, permed and highlighted hair—and help him create a more sophisticated image. This would help him to fit in with the preppy, collegiate look of the high-fashion world into which he had entered.

"You don't seem shy and introverted to me. Do you mind if I ask where you work?"

"I work in a hair salon. I'm a hair-stylist."

Renee's eyes widened. "Oh, my gosh, we have a hair salon here! Are you happy at your current salon?"

"Are you kidding me? I hate it there. My boss and I aren't exactly best friends. It was my first job out of hair school and after two years, it is not going well. "

"We're looking for a new stylist. Do you think you might be interested?"

Renee and Thomas both marveled at the stroke of serendipity.

Thomas stood straight up, threw back his shoulders, and proclaimed, "Yes, I am interested. I would love to work here, Renee."

"Wonderful. You can start immediately, and I'm sure we can help you overcome your shyness. Maybe you've just been at the wrong place all this time. Let me show you around."

Renee showed him around the complex, certain that anyone who met him would be impressed with her new find. She showed him the school, the salon and the photography studio, and introduced him to the owner of the agency. He met the other stylists, makeup artists, and their in-house photographer.

Although Thomas Paul's enthusiasm for the modeling world was unyielding and infectious, he was never comfortable in front of the camera. On the outside, he seemed destined for success, but internally he struggled with a lack of confidence. He lacked that gregarious, outgoing nature needed to truly make it in the modeling business. There were brief moments where he felt he could play the part, but they were few and far between and seemed to be out of his control. Still, he excelled in the salon. He was constantly stimulated in his new environment; so much so that his personality began to flower as he immersed himself, undaunted, into his new career of beauty and fashion.

*   *   *

"Thomas Paul Stanton." Thomas jumped in his seat as he heard his name boom over the intercom. He felt himself blush, as if he had done something wrong. He worried that every other person knew just how lost he felt in an airport. He remained in his seat and waited.

"Mr. Thomas Paul Stanton. Please report to the information desk to meet the rest of your party," a pleasant female voice announced.

"Thank God," he said out loud to nobody in particular. Relieved that his friends were looking for him, he set out to find them. As he passed the men's room, his mind started to wander.

Thomas parked the car in the lot at the airport, stepped out onto the pavement, locked the door, and headed inside. With nervous eyes, he looked around at all the people milling about with luggage. His motives for being at the airport that day were simple enough. Thomas was in search of a teenage sexual outlet. Frustrated by not knowing where to meet other gay people, he was resorting to this clandestine pit stop in hopes that something he heard once at a party might be true. Did gay people really hang out in the bathrooms at the airport?

Thomas Paul, his heart thumping in his chest, looked at the nameless faces surrounding him, and someone caught his eye. A young guy, about his age, dressed in a t-shirt and shorts, stood against the wall a few feet away, staring at him. Thomas glanced back. His mouth felt dry and his palms were sweaty. Thomas looked a second time and again; the young man returned his gaze and then offered a subtle, almost imperceptible nod towards the bathroom.

Anxious, Thomas made his way to the bathroom and glanced over his shoulder to see if he was being followed. Instinctively, he walked up to the urinal, and moments later the stranger sidled up next to him. Thomas gazed down and noticed the young man's penis. He was shocked to find that they were both aroused.

He had been repulsed by the priest's genitalia and worried that the experiences with Father Bob had corrupted him forever. He regularly fantasized about having sex with other guys but wondered if and when the time actually came if the nakedness of another guy would sicken him.

Neither of them spoke as Thomas, shaking with excitement, followed the stranger into a stall. The difference between this and what had happened with Father Bob was so immense, Thomas couldn't describe it. To be doing something sexual with a peer, with someone he found attractive, changed everything. Regardless of the guilt he felt and the seediness of it, he was overcome with pleasure.

Later, as he drove home, he felt ashamed but relieved that he had finally had consensual sex and had enjoyed it. Despite being forced into a three-foot stall at an airport, he was euphoric.

For months he would return to the airport looking for the young man but never saw him again.

"There you are! God, we were starting to worry. Come on, we're about to board soon," Renee said. She grabbed Thomas by the hand and led the way through security.

Thomas Paul bubbled with enthusiasm as they made their way down the jet way to the plane. The array of smells was dizzying: fresh coffee brewing, jet fuel, cigarette smoke, perfume, and fast food from greasy bags being carried on. It was a thrilling moment.

"Ladies and gentlemen, our flight will not be full tonight. Please feel free to move about the cabin and sit where you choose," the stewardess announced over the intercom.

Thomas chose a row of seats behind Renee and looked around with hungry eyes. He flicked open the armrest ashtray over and over, like a child in awe. Click. Click. Click. Click.

Renee turned around and looked at him.

"I never want this to end!" He smiled, mesmerized by the whole experience of flying for the first time. He buckled his seat belt tightly and lit a cigarette to calm his nerves as he looked out the small window and waited. He smoked quickly, to be sure he was finished before the non-smoking light flashed.

The engines roared to life and the plane taxied down the runway. Thomas gripped the armrests with sweaty palms, and as the plane lunged forward and took off, the pressure pushed him back into his seat.

"Hey, Renee, I think I want to be a pilot. This is the best roller-coaster ride I have ever been on!" His friends and a few strangers laughed—his excitement was contagious.

After a couple of hours, Thomas felt a tap on his shoulder. "Thomas, look." Renee pointed out the window. He looked out and a lump formed in his throat as he glimpsed the nighttime Manhattan skyline.

This is the biggest, most beautiful sight I have ever seen. As he stared out the window, his eyes were wet with tears. He looked over at Renee, who was smiling at him.

"I don't think I have ever been this happy." He was twenty-three years old.

Click was affiliated with Elite Modeling Agency in New York City and as hosts, Elite had provided the Click group with a black, stretch limo to take them from their hotel to Studio 54. Thomas had to pinch himself. *Please don't let this be a dream.*

They waited together outside the club, packed in the crowd like sardines, wearing their Elite t-shirts, which they had cut up with scissors to follow the latest fashion trend. Throngs of people stood in line waiting to be hand-picked by the doorman and granted permission to enter. Unaware of what was going on, he felt Renee pushing him forward.

"Go! He's waving you over," she said smiling.

He looked back at her in confusion.

'Don't worry, we'll be in soon. Go! It's 'cause you're gorgeous. Be flattered."

He walked into the club and felt the throbbing beat of the music vibrate through his body. He had to force himself to keep his mouth from dropping open. It was unlike any of the clubs he had seen at home.

Studio 54 was an old theater, which had been converted into the most popular and well-known discotheque of all time. The cavernous dance floor was the entire first level of the building, surrounded by bars, lounges and private rooms. Thomas stood speechless as his senses absorbed the multitude of sights, sounds and smells.

In the blink of an eye the dance floor went dark, and huge, thirty-foot, cylindrical towers of lights descended from the ceiling onto the floor, setting off an intricate light show that was beyond dazzling. Thomas stood in anticipation, wondering what would come next. Then, a suspended catwalk started moving back and forth. Next, to the sound of thunder, The Weather Girls, who were perched on the platform, started singing. As they belted out their classic hit, *It's Raining Men*, confetti, water droplets, and glitter showered the now crazed dancers, cheering below. Thomas was awestruck by the show and by the crowd of beautiful people dancing under the strobe lights.

He surveyed the dance floor and noticed that his light hair, blue eyes and fair complexion made him stand out from the dark-haired, dark-skinned, dark-eyed myriad of ethnic people who dominated the population of NYC. He could see many of them, men and women, looking at him with approval.

In contrast to his teenage years, he realized that he was being looked at in a good way. It was New York City—where all things were accepted! They were all here. Straight, gay, men, women, black, white, and everything in between. He was in his element.

A drink appeared in his hand out of nowhere, followed by the sound of a deep voice behind him.

"Hey, hot stuff, you want a cocktail?"

There was no hesitation on Thomas Paul's part as the stranger with the deep voice ushered him onto the dance floor.

It's raining men! Hallelujah indeed.

He was in heaven.

The next morning, hungover and exhausted but happy, Thomas waited with the others by the hotel elevator, impatiently watching the floor numbers decline until it reached the lobby. The doors opened and without lifting his head, Thomas shuffled into the elevator car and bumped into someone. He looked up and gasped.

Kathy Daniels was still the most beautiful girl he had ever seen. Her eyes were pale hazel-green and as big as a doe's, with lashes that fluttered and reached her brows when she blinked. Her lips were full and round, with a small scar on the lower one that only served to make them look more pouty. Her nose was small and delicate and her skin, flawless. Her hair was long and naturally blonde. She was tall, sophisticated and feminine and one of the most striking and photogenic girls at Click — an *A* girl, destined for New York. And now she was here, standing in front of him at The Blackstone Hotel in Manhattan.

Months before, back at home, she had flirted with him, and he had not been immune to it. But not long after meeting her, she left for New York. In his mind, he had accepted that he was gay and that his girlfriend days were over. Surely, girls would figure it out too.

"Oh, my God, Thomas Paul!" Kathy threw her arms around him. "I didn't know you'd be here. It's great to see a familiar face."

They hugged and stepped off the elevator amidst the throngs of people clamoring to get on. Thomas was dumbfounded to see her and feel her touch.

"I have to run — test shoot — but make sure you find me later I want to talk to you." She kissed him on the cheek and was gone as quickly as she had appeared. Thomas shook his head, wondering if he had really seen her or if he was still a little drunk from the night before.

He was glad to have seen her. Gay or not, sexual or not, his attraction to her was overwhelming. Maybe it was just the attention of someone that popular and beautiful. Whatever the reason, he could not ignore his feelings. It was a nice surprise at the end of an unforgettable trip. He thought of her often on the plane ride home. Perhaps there was still a chance for him. Maybe he was normal, after all.

*   *   *

Weeks later, the phone rang at the salon. "Hi, Thomas, can you guess who this is?" asked a soft, breathy, female voice spoke on the other end.

"I'm afraid I can't, but did you need an appointment?"

"Yes, I do," the voice was coy, "but not to get my hair done." She laughed. "It's Kathy Daniels. I waited for you to call but you never did, so I'm calling you. I thought maybe we could get together."

"I'd love to see you, Kathy. Give me your number and I'll call after work tonight."

They went to the park on their first date and spent the day walking and talking. He could sense she was attracted to him, and it boosted his confidence. They came upon a swing set and Kathy sat in one of the swings. Thomas stood in front of her and pulled her close to him. They kissed and her lips were soft and sweet. His kiss was deep, strong and intimate and she responded, not like some girls who cautioned him to be gentler. She pulled him closer and kissed him back with intensity. "Thomas, I am so attracted to you. I hoped for so long that you would call, but you never did."

"I'm sorry, Kathy. I'm just shy but I'm even more attracted to you." While chuckling at his comment, they kissed again and at that moment, that afternoon, they fell in love.

They dated and met each other's parents and spent countless hours making out and exploring one another. Soon, the modeling world come calling for her again, and although she was upset to be leaving him, he was relieved. Thomas was painfully aware that his body was not functioning the way it should during their make-out sessions. He was sure she was aware of it—he could sense her silent questioning when she looked into his eyes. It was time.

"Kathy, there is something I need to tell you." They were leaning against the car in the driveway of her parents' house.

She turned to look at him. "I knew it. You've met someone else."

"No, there's no one else, Kathy. It's ..." He hesitated. "I'm bi-sexual." It was the only explanation he was brave enough to admit to her, or to himself.

Telling her the whole truth, that for years now, his sexual attraction to girls had waned to an almost non-existent state would be humiliating after having gone this far with her. Emotionally, he was always able to develop powerful bonds with girls, but it ended there. Any physical attraction he felt was a deep appreciation for their beauty but didn't evoke a trace of sexual stimulation. He was tortured over his conflicting feelings, which were now fully out of his control.

Silence.

She began to cry. "I thought it was because you had lost interest in me. You never get, you know," she shrugged, "hard, when you lie on top of me. I thought there was somebody else."

"I'm sorry I kept it from you. I didn't know how to tell you," Thomas said.

"Well, at least I can stop blaming myself." Her tears turned to sobs. "Have you met a guy?"

"No. I have never met anyone like you, Kathy, and I love you so much." He took her in his arms. "But I had to tell you before we went any further."

"You mean you want to keep seeing me?" she asked, sniffling.

"Yes. I just couldn't let you go to Europe without knowing the truth."

"But how can I trust you, Thomas? I mean, I can compete with other girls but, guys? You will eventually want to be with one." Her tone was defeated.

"Kathy, if two people really love each other, they have to commit to one another. Then everything else, including my hard-on, will work out. There is nothing in the world I want more than to be with you. I love you, not someone else. Girl or guy. Only you!"

She stared at him and her crying had ceased.

"I need time. I don't know what to say. I know I love you, too, but I have a lot to think about. I'll call you when I figure things out, okay?"

During the next few days, he made numerous attempts to call her, but his calls went unanswered. Finally, after a week, she called him.

"I leave for Germany early tomorrow. I don't know what will happen while I'm gone, but I do know that I love you and when I get back, we're going to be together and try and make it work."

It was not meant to be. She eventually returned but never called. Time passed. They realized their love affair was spoiled by something neither of them could control, and they both moved on.

She was his last girlfriend.

For years, Thomas would wade aimlessly through an ocean of meaningless sexual encounters with forgotten men, always hoping one of them would be the one to fulfill his growing desire for long-term companionship.

Despite his rewarding professional life, he found himself desperate and alone, just as he had been in his younger years. Hoping to relieve his loneliness, he remembered a new client whom he had bonded with and who might be able to help him.

It would be the beginning of a life-changing journey.

PART
TWO

Chapter 18

First Therapy Session 1987

Susan Murphy smoothed out her skirt and picked up a yellow, legal notepad. In her other hand, she held a large, exquisite pen and waited, poised to write. "Alright, Thomas, tell me why you're here today." She smiled.

Where to begin? he thought to himself. He looked around the room. Susan's office was large, and the furnishings were sumptuous and comfortable. Her massive desk and the coffee and end tables, along with the wall of bookshelves behind her desk, were made of dark cherry wood. The couch, two chairs placed at each end of the couch, and Susan's own tall, swivel, office chair, were covered in thick, dark green leather. Most empty spaces in the room were filled with shiny, thriving plants of all species and sizes.

Thomas Paul smiled back at Susan. *You've come this far. It's time. Tell her everything.*

"It might surprise you to know that I'm not always the happy, funny, talkative man you see when you sit in my stylist's chair."

"I may have just started my career, Thomas, but I think very little of what you may tell me will surprise me. Trust me."

Thomas nodded. "I do trust you. That's why I'm here."

"I'm glad," Susan said.

He took a deep breath and continued.

"I don't think I like life as much as other people do." Thomas paused, searching Susan's eyes.

"Can you explain that for me?"

"I often think of taking my own life when things don't feel right on the inside."

True to her word, Susan showed no emotion at the revelation that her newest client voiced that he had suicidal thoughts. "How often do you think of taking your life?" She asked as she put her pen to paper.

"Sometimes every day—since I was a teenager. But I want to be like everyone else. Like the people I hear all the time, saying they love their lives and love living. I want to value life too — my life."

Susan asked, "What is it that you feel, that makes you *think* you want to take your life?"

"I think it's when I feel afraid that I am never going to be loved, or when I think people don't like me. That if it gets too lonely for too long, I have an escape."

"Have you ever felt you could go through with it?" Susan's voice showed concern.

"I tried once when I was a teenager, but not since. Sometimes it's more like...I just wish I were dead." "Do you actually have it planned if things get that tough?"

"No. It may sound strange but after that failed attempt, I feel like I am supposed to be alive. Do people really love living?" 'Of course they do."

"I don't understand how. Between fear, rejection, disappointment, loneliness, isolation, and so many other things, what is there to make you want to go on?"

The words poured out of him. "I have no children, I have strained relationships with my family, I don't feel like I have any real value and worst of all, I feel tossed aside and forgotten."

Susan nodded as she listened.

"Sometimes I wish I would get cancer or just suddenly drop over dead. And since that isn't happening, I think 'why not just do it myself'?"

"But you know that's not the answer, don't you?"

"I know that's what people say. Happy people. And I know people say suicide is cowardly, but it's not cowardice. It's despair and an act of total desperation."

Susan finished writing and looked up at him. Thomas Paul's eyes were moist as they met hers. "Will it ever go away?" he asked.

"Yes," she answered firmly.

Thomas sniffled and chuckled. "Well, it's a good thing this couch is so comfortable because I have a feeling I will be spending a bit of time on it." He pulled a tissue from the box on the coffee table. He'd noticed the box upon entering her office that morning and thought it seemed cliché. Now, as he dabbed at his eyes during his very first session, he wondered just how often she actually had to replace it.

"This is all new to me—therapy. Do you know how intrigued and then relieved I was when you sat in the salon and told me you were a therapist?" he said.

"I'm glad to be able to help and honored that you trust me, Thomas."

"And I'm honored that you trust me with your hair." They chuckled in unison.

"Are you ready to continue?"

"Absolutely."

"Good you've told me there are a few areas in your life that are causing you concern. You should know that your thoughts of suicide and desperation are not that uncommon, and you have taken a big step towards healing in simply seeking me out and admitting your pain. I commend you for that."

"Thank you."

"Is there anything else you'd care to share with me to help me put some pieces together?"

He was eager to open up to her. "Well, I've never had a long lasting relationship and I am twenty-seven years old. It just all seems to be a bunch of meaningless sexual encounters with people I meet and end up not caring about. Some of them I even come to really dislike." He was unaware that what he was really trying to explain to her was that most of his sexual experiences felt deviant to him. "I can have almost anyone I want and have, but I don't want to do that anymore, especially now with AIDS. I've spent quite a bit of time traveling between New York and Miami and believe me, in those cities it seems like it's spreading as fast as fleas jump from one dog to another. The entire gay community has been branded as the center of God's punishment and that His way of showing it is by killing us for our evil ways.

You can't even kiss a guy now for fear of dying a horrible death, with everyone pointing their fingers at you and hating you, even when you're sick. It's terrifying, Susan, and now most of us are convinced that we *are* the devil's plague — all because of our sexual orientation. I WISH I COULD NOT BE GAY. But I have tried everything to change it and am sick of hating myself for it!

I want to meet the right guy and stop sleeping around, but I just can't seem to do that. When I meet someone it seems so right, and I go for it. But then, mostly, it turns out so wrong." He looked up at her. "I don't know what's wrong with me."

Susan leaned forward in a gesture of support. "I'm not sure anything is wrong with you, Thomas. Understanding the reasons why we are the way are, or do the things we do, is a critical part of our developmental process. Taking responsibility for our actions and not allowing those reasons to turn into excuses for continuing unwanted behavior is what counts. Just your being here is a great first step towards making a change, Thomas. There is something else you should know that will ease your mind. The CDC has confirmed that the HIV virus, which causes AIDS, cannot be detected in saliva." She smiled at him. "This means you can kiss whomever you like and rest easy knowing that you won't die from it."

Thomas Paul's eyebrows were raised. "Are you sure? I've heard that but, I didn't know if I could believe it."

She nodded. "Yes, I'm sure. Now, let's move on." Her pen and legal pad were at the ready. "When was the last time you were truly happy?" she asked without looking up.

Thomas Paul thought for a moment. "I don't think I know how to be happy. I know I was depressed when I was younger and although I don't think I'm depressed anymore, I often feel dead on the inside. And I think I learned to be unhappy because that is what they taught me."

"Who taught you?"

"My parents."

"Why do you think they taught you to be unhappy?"

"Because they were unhappy and I didn't live in a happy family. I may be wrong, but I do think it has a lot to do with why I am the way I am."

Susan nodded. "You are very probably correct."

Thomas felt thoughts and words come to his mind faster than he could get them out of his mouth. "No matter how many times they told us they loved us, they never seemed to act like they really did. They always taught us to let our actions, not our words, speak for us—but that rule didn't apply to them. Their actions showed us that they were miserable despite trying to tell us the opposite with their meaningless words."

Susan kept writing and nodding but did not look up or speak and her silence encouraged him to continue.

"I tried to learn Spanish for years in school but I never caught on. I even liked Spanish class but no matter how hard I tried, it just wouldn't stick. It was *so* hard! And I feel like it's the same thing with being happy. No matter how much I want to be, I just can't seem to get it. Just like I never became fluent in Spanish, I don't think I will ever become fluent in happy."

Susan smiled and kept writing. Finally, she looked up from the notepad. "That was quite a powerful analogy. You are a very astute young man."

I am? he thought to himself.

Thomas covered his mouth with his hand. "But am I talking too much? Should I be letting you talk more? You are supposed to tell me what's wrong with me, right?"

Susan shook her head. "Not at all—you are here for self-discovery. I am merely a guide for you to discover things on your own and so far, you are off to a great start. Believe it or not, the answers are inside you, Thomas. I'm just here to help you unlock them." She smiled. "Never censor yourself in front of me. Don't ever feel like you are saying too much. There is never too much shared in therapy. Every little bit will help me to help you."

Thomas laughed. "Phew! Okay. I feel so at ease with you I just want to let it all out."

"That's wonderful. You have been right on with your words except for one thing. You can and will come to be fluent in happy if you really want to be. But it is a process, not an event."

"I'm ready."

"As adults, we are all responsible for our own happiness and you have taken a very big first step in finally finding yours. Through our work together, you can learn to change your life and no longer let your past influence your present and more importantly, your future."

Thomas was comforted by her words. It had been so long since he'd had an ally, that he had almost forgotten the feeling.

"We have some time left. Do you feel up to continuing?"

"I'm open to whatever you ask of me," Thomas replied.

"Alright, let's go back a bit and start at the beginning." Her face was calm and encouraging. "Tell me more about your family."

Tell me more about your family. It was a simple request, but the answer, much more complex.

"Well, like I've talked about when you've come for hair appointments, my mom and dad are still married, and I have three siblings. My older brother, one older sister, and a younger sister."

"Good, let's start there. So, how are your relationships with your parents?" she prodded, eyes steady on her note pad.

Thomas shrugged. "Somewhat strained, I guess."

"How so?"

Thomas watched her pen fly across the paper as he spoke. "My father was a loving but militaristic, impatient, abusive tyrant. I'm his gay, hairdresser son. When I was eighteen, he asked me if I was a queer. I lied. He knows I'm gay now, but we don't speak about it. It's kind of like — don't ask, don't tell."

Susan kept writing.

"My mother has suffered on and off with mental illness since I was a young boy. She is the neediest woman on earth and also pretty sick physically. I love her but she wasn't there much for me as a child when I really needed her."

Susan stopped writing and looked up. "Okay, let's stop here for a moment before you continue on to other family members. Your mother ... let's focus on her for now."

Thomas nodded. "Sure."

"To what mental illness are you referring?" *Has she actually been diagnosed and treated for mental illness?*

He went on to tell her everything he could think of. How she was once so beautiful and so attentive to his needs and then for so many reasons, many of which he still couldn't fully understand, she became a fragile, empty shell of her former self.

The hysterectomy that seemed to have started it all, soiling the furniture and herself in the throes of temporary insanity, the doctors, the pills, the breakdowns, the blackouts, the hospitalizations, and her general incapacity to deal with anything while her husband worked away from home five days a week for most of their entire marriage.

Susan scribbled with fury, and Thomas could detect an almost hunger-like look on her face. She was new to the profession but already, in the little time that she had spent with him, she knew what she had in front of her. Thomas Paul Stanton might very well be the biggest task of her career. She was realistic to the challenge that lay ahead.

"Therapy is never easy, Thomas Paul. And like life itself, you will get out of it as much as you are willing to put into it."

"I understand."

"Before we end our session today, I want to say one more thing. When we meet, I need you to be truthful at all times. Not being truthful will only lead to roadblocks in your path to healing, so I am asking for your total honesty during our sessions. If you're comfortable with that, I'd like to start meeting twice a week."

"Absolutely. But..."

"Is there a problem?" she asked.

"I'd like to come twice a week, but I don't know if I can afford it."

"Don't worry about the money for now. As long as you pay me something every month, I'll keep track of our appointments ,and we will deal with it later, okay?"

"Okay."

Chapter 19

Second Month of Therapy

"What is the first word that comes to your mind when I mention your father?"

"Tyrant. I hated the son of a bitch," Thomas said without hesitation.

"Was he always that way?"

"I guess not, but that is what I remember most. We just never knew what would set him off."

"What about good times, happy memories?"

Thomas shrugged. "Yeah, there were some. When I was really young, he wasn't so short-tempered. But then…"

"Then what?"

"I guess the older I got, the less he liked me."

Susan listened and had not started writing yet.

"Do you really think he treated you differently than your siblings?"

"Yes, at times. I was not what he wanted in a son. I wasn't athletic like my brother and I was...different. He knew it. Everybody knew it."

"You mentioned that he was not so impatient when you were younger. Why do you think that?"

"I dunno."

"He worked out of town then, didn't he?"

"Yes, every week of pretty much my entire childhood. I never understood why we annoyed him so much when he hardly ever saw us."

"What do you think changed as you got older? Why do you think he was more impatient?" Susan looked him in the eye as he thought about her question.

Thomas raised his shoulders in confusion. "I don't know."

"Think, Thomas. I think you take too much credit for your father's abusive moods and anger. I want you to look back through the eyes of the adult you are now and not as the child you were then. Can you remove yourself from the picture and look at your family objectively?"

Thomas closed his eyes for a moment.

"What do you see when you look back at your father?" she asked.

"He left us. He left us with her!"

"With who?" Susan had stopped writing again.

"With my mother—my crazy, sick, incompetent mother. For five days a week we were alone with her and that meant alone, on our own! We were just kids. And when he came back, he didn't even have the decency to wonder how hard that must have been for us—fending for ourselves, hungry, dirty, and confused. We needed him to relieve the burden, but he just made it worse by forcing us to tip-toe around in fear of getting a boot in the ass if we stepped out of line."

"This is good, Thomas. Let it out."

"Angry. He was angry all the time and he didn't know how to deal with it. When he was angry, he hit. He yelled, screamed, threatened, called us names, or put his fists through walls or doors and then he would say 'I was angry and couldn't help it,' like that was supposed to excuse his behavior."

"Does all this make you angry now?" she asked.

"Yes. I was angry then, too, but anger doesn't give you a license to hurt anyone. Even though I have wanted to many times. I don't scream and punch people or things, nor do I want to. Everybody in my house did that for most of my life and it doesn't solve anything. It never made anything better. No matter how much I want to give in to my anger, I try to talk about it and work it out."

Susan listened and nodded.

Thomas Paul sighed. "All we wanted was for him to love us. And to help us. Help us with *her*. We didn't want him to leave all the time but he did. He always left." Thomas Paul's eyes were moist with tears.

"Do you think it was easy for him to leave?" Susan asked.

"How could it not have been? He did it every week!"

"I know you're angry and your feelings are justified. This is all really good but I want you to think about it. Why do you think he left every week?"

Thomas looked Susan in the eye.

"Because he wanted to get away from her too." Susan nodded.

"And the sicker she became, the angrier he got. But he didn't feel right taking it out on her so he took it out on us instead, rationalizing it as discipline." Thomas spoke to himself as much as he spoke to Susan.

"Do you think they loved each other?" Susan asked.

"Yes." Thomas did not hesitate in answering. "Well, he loved her. But she ended up hating him."

"Why do you think that?"

"She was young, beautiful, and naïve, and he saddled her with four kids and then left her to raise them alone. And it made her crazy, which made him angry. Then he stayed away because she was crazy, and his absence made her worse. I see it now, another part of the cycle."

Again, Susan nodded but said nothing.

"She tried to punish him."

"How so?" Susan asked.

"She had affairs. When I was fourteen, she told me that I am not his biological son."

Susan resumed writing but showed no expression on her face. "How did that make you feel at the time?"

"Great. I was happy. I used to dream about my real father, that one day we would meet and he would love me and be so proud of me. The fantasy sustained me for a while," Thomas said.

"And how do you feel about it now?"

"I don't know. It was so long ago I don't really think about it anymore. It doesn't change anything."

"Are you sure?" Susan asked.

Thomas was silent for a moment.

"Don't underestimate the effects of such a revelation, Thomas. It is normal and understandable for you to feel hurt and confused by it. It may have given you some comfort, knowing that the man who raised you but abused you is not your flesh and blood. But he was the only father you knew. You still wanted him to love you and accept you."

Thomas nodded and felt relief from her words.

"It is a lot to deal with, the myriad of conflicting emotions that come along with a secret like that."

"You're right. I thought it was no big deal but maybe it was. Maybe it is," Thomas said.

"Do you think your father ever knew the truth?" Susan asked.

"No. But telling me the secret sure made my mother feel better. I know now that when she told me, it was her way of hurting him, even if he didn't know it."

"How do you feel about your father now?" Susan asked.

"I don't know. Like I said, there was happiness in our household and in part his discipline helped make me the man I am today, but it would have been better not to have been beaten into submission, living in constant fear."

"You have come full circle today." Susan smiled as she spoke.

"I guess. My relationship with my dad is by no means perfect."

"The important thing for you to remember is that, like many men of his generation, he did as much as he was able to do. Nobody teaches people how to parent. They just follow the lead from their own parents, never questioning if the things they are doing are right or wrong. And much of what your father felt had little to do with you and your siblings. He was struggling with himself and with his own feelings as much as anything and probably still is today," Susan surmised.

"Do you think he ever feels guilty?" Thomas asked.

"I don't know your father. What do you think? In the end, does it matter? Would his guilt help you?"

"Shouldn't it? I mean, it would be nice to think he was remorseful for subjecting us to his uncontrolled tyrannical rages, his verbal attacks, and his abandoning us."

"Possibly. But my goal here is for you to learn to love yourself and to know that you were and *are* deserving of love, kindness, and respect because you're a good person and a fine man all on your own — not because others, family or not, feel that you are. Once you believe that, everything else in your life will fall into place."

"But how can I love myself if I don't feel like anyone else does?" Thomas asked.

Susan laughed. "That's the whole point, my friend. If everyone had to wait to be loved before they could love themselves and love others, it would be a very lonely world. You have to love yourself first."

Thomas looked doubtful.

"It's okay." Susan smiled. "I'm here and I'm going to help you do it. You can trust me, remember?"

"I do," he said.

Chapter 20

Third Month of Therapy

Susan leaned back in her chair, her hands folded in her lap. "I think it's time to talk some more about your mother, Thomas."

She waited and studied Thomas Paul's expression.

"I hated that pathetic fucking woman," he spat.

"Do you really think you hated her?"

"I'm pretty fucking sure I know who the fuck I hated!'

Susan did not respond.

"She was a lazy, sick, mean, depressed, dirty fucking pig. You would have hated her, too! I had to wait on her lazy ass hand and foot all the fucking time. She never did a goddamned thing for herself—in her whole fucking life. Only thing she ever did was say she loved us, but it never meant shit because she never did anything to prove it! I spent all my time taking care of her, and I don't even care that I walked out and left her fat ass when I did."

Susan exhaled. "You sound very angry, Thomas. You're speaking in a way that I've heard you speak a few times before, but I don't think it's the Thomas I've come to know." Again, she waited for his reaction, but he merely looked at her. "Maybe it was just a part of you who hated her."

"What are you talking about?" he asked.

"Children who have been traumatized, particularly when the trauma is ongoing for a length of time, can subconsciously develop different parts of their personality. These other parts respond to and help that person cope with situations that they normally couldn't deal with on their own because they haven't developed those coping skills yet."

The tiny hairs on the back of his neck came to life and his skin prickled with a slow awakening. "Oh," he replied.

Susan waited for a moment before continuing again. "Just for fun, let's give a name to the part of you who is angry and acts out in hatred. If we can separate these different parts of your personality, and name them, it may help you sort through and understand some of the feelings that may be causing you problems in your relationships with others. Does that sound like something you'd like to do?"

"I guess, but I'm almost twenty-eight years old and this seems silly." Susan smiled. "It may seem silly but I really think it will help. Why don't you play along, okay? What would you like to name him?" she prodded.

Thomas shrugged. "Okay. How about Eagle?"

"Good. Why do you think you chose Eagle?" she asked.

"Cause eagles are fierce, all-seeing, and can swoop down on their prey, kill and fly away when they want. They can protect you, too."

"Does that make you feel powerful?"

"Yes!" Thomas said.

"I'm glad you feel empowered, Thomas. Do you think Eagle protects you?"

"What do you mean?"

"We all have a child in us who, to a greater or lesser degree, needs to feel protected. I'm not sure that the boy inside of you ever really felt, much less was, protected. Did Eagle become your protector?" Susan asked.

Thomas hesitated for a moment and pondered her words. "I guess, maybe."

"Is Eagle dangerous? Should I be afraid of him? Would he try to hurt anybody?"

"No." Thomas shook his head. "I don't think so, especially not you."

Susan smiled. "That's good, Thomas. Can you tell me how old Eagle is?"

Thomas frowned. "I don't know what you mean."

"How old were you when you first started getting angry and speaking in the way you spoke to me today?

Thomas looked up at the ceiling and thought about her question. "Maybe sixteen."

"Then let's say that Eagle is about sixteen. He probably developed many years ago, to help protect "little Thomas" from danger. He has become a part of your personality and he comes out when you feel threatened."

As she spoke, a cacophony of bells sounded in his head. It all resonated with him and was starting to make sense. Finally, he was beginning to understand.

She continued. "In your life now, since you are an adult and on your own, there is no longer reason for you to feel threatened ,and Eagle may be causing some of your problems. He is still sixteen, and in time we may try to help him grow up a little."

Thomas nodded.

Susan leaned forward on her desk. "Did you love your mother?"

Thomas was calm. "I wanted to. But I don't think I ever had a mother. She never did anything for me."

Susan smiled again. "That's better, Thomas. Do you want to feel better about your mother?"

"Yes, I think so."

"Can you try and remember pleasant memories of a healthier, more nurturing mom?"

"I could try. I have tried, but I don't know how. I was always afraid of her."

Thomas Paul's eyes watered and his thoughts drifted back to a childhood memory.

It was bubblegum pink, fragrant, and sweet on his tongue. He could almost taste it right here and now as he sat on Susan's couch, as if someone had just offered him a soft, fresh piece. The delicate, airy bubble was big and round, almost the size of his face. He was so proud of it, as any nine-year-old child mastering the fine art of bubblegum blowing would be. But the eventual pop was unavoidable, and the sticky residue covered his lips, cheeks, and nose. He picked off as much as he could and went about his day, the leftover goo collecting dirt and grime as the afternoon wore on.

He walked into the house to find his mother dressed up and in heels, her hair freshly set and shiny. She was pressing her lips together to set her lipstick when she spotted him in the kitchen, a crusty black film of dried gum on his face. Her eyes widened and her pink lips formed an angry snarl. She reached for him and dug her fingernails into his face.

"What is that all over your face?"

Thomas Paul was frightened, not knowing what he had done to make her angry. "I don't know." His eyes were as wide as hers, and he winced as she scraped her nails down his cheeks with swift, sharp stabs in an attempt to clean the gum off.

She grabbed his face in her hand and raised her voice in anger and frustration. "Why, why, why did I ever have you ungrateful little fuckers in the first place? Nothing I do makes you kids behave like you're supposed to. I swear, Thomas Paul, if you make me break one of my fucking fingernails, you'll be sorry."

Of course he was afraid. There was nowhere to go, nowhere to run. He was a child, trapped and forced to endure any kind of punishment or discipline for any reason that his parents saw fit. But it wasn't the punishments that scared him the most. It was the unknown—never knowing when they would snap and lash out.

Thomas Paul was unable to tell the difference between right and wrong. The smallest, most innocent thing seemed, so often, to be bad.

But she loved him. She told him so, over and over. They both did, instilling in him the belief that violence and fear were all part of the process of loving. So to endure, Thomas Paul withdrew inside himself. That was his modus operandi. Until little by little, he stopped feeling anything. He trusted no one. People who loved you hurt you just as much as people who didn't. Soon he could no longer tell friend from foe and could not find his way back out to who he once was.

"Thomas, do you still trust me?" Susan's voice awoke him from his reverie.

"Of course."

"Good. If you agree, on our next visit, we could try hypnosis. If you are receptive, it could help you remember a younger mother who wasn't always so sick and may have been able to love you a little better."

Thomas nodded. "I'll try."

Susan smiled and was ready to end the session.

"Susan, I'm desperate. Have you ever heard of those children who have no pain sensors and don't know they're bleeding because they can't feel when they've been cut?"

She nodded as she listened, encouraging him to continue.

"I feel that way on the inside—like I have been bleeding to death emotionally but didn't know it because I didn't know I was being hurt." His voice trailed off.

"That is because you are so conditioned to being wounded, Thomas. You have come to accept the pain that you feel from being hurt is normal."

He looked at her.

"I'm always here for you. I will help you learn to heal yourself, and to feel again."

He believed her and had faith in her, more than he'd ever had in anyone else in his life.

Chapter 21

Sixth Month of Therapy

"How are you feeling today, Thomas? You don't seem yourself."

He laughed and reclined on the sofa. "You know me so well now. I had a rough night."

Susan smiled. "Whatever did you find to do on a Wednesday night in this town?"

"Just went to one of the bars. It was hump night so there were drink specials. Not too bad of a crowd for a Wednesday."

"Well, unless you have something specific you want to talk about today, why don't we talk about that?" Susan offered.

"Sure. What do you want to know?"

"How about we start with your telling me why it was rough."

"Sometimes when I go out, I drink more than I want to and last night was one of those nights." He laughed again.

Susan picked up her pen and started writing. "How often do you do that?"

Thomas shrugged. "Just depends on how I'm feeling on any given night."

"Do you think you have a problem with alcohol, Thomas?"

"I dunno. Do you think I have a problem with alcohol?" he asked in return.

"Well...how often do you drink?"

"Usually only when I go out, maybe two or three times a week."

"Do you always drink too much?" Susan asked.

"No."

"You've told me in the past that you don't take any prescription medications, but what about recreational drugs?"

Thomas sat up on the couch and focused on her questions. *Total honesty.*

"I've tried cocaine and acid, but it always makes me feel bad. I'll pop a valium if I can get my hands on one, and I like to smoke pot."

"And how often do you do that?"

"If I have it, every day."

"How many times a day do you smoke?" Susan looked down at the ever-present legal pad as she questioned him and documented his answers.

"Morning, noon, and night until it's all gone."

"Are there ever times when you don't smoke marijuana?"

"Nope. Not if I have it on me."

"Do you smoke before our sessions?" Thomas was glad she did not look up from her writing. "Oh no, I wouldn't do that," he lied. It was the only time he had ever lied to her.

Susan's tone was serious when she answered. "I would hope not, and I would like you to promise me that you won't get high before our sessions."

"I'll try." He felt guilty for lying to her. She trusted him. He told himself he wouldn't smoke pot before seeing her.

"I suppose that's a good-enough answer. Let's continue. When you drink too much, what do you think makes you do that?"

"I don't know. Sometimes I go out and keep to myself because I'm so shy and awkward. I'm afraid to go up to strangers even though I hate being alone. I feel very self-conscious and nearly paralyzed with fear. Often, if someone does approach, I freeze up and don't know what to say—then get called arrogant and stuck-up. But there are times that I feel different. I go out and it's like I'm someone else. I'm not afraid of people. I can approach them and not struggle with what to say. I wish I could be that outgoing person all the time! He is always fun and friendly and happy and has never met a stranger. I have so much more fun when I'm like that."

"Do you drink more when you are the shy person or when you are the outgoing person?"

"Oh, definitely, when I am feeling great! I'm having so much fun, and it just seems like drinking more makes it even better," he said laughing.

Susan stopped writing. "Well, not everyone who drinks too much is an alcoholic. Drinking and using drugs can just turn into a bad habit for some people. There are definite signs and symptoms of true alcoholism. Do you know what they are?"

"You mean besides getting shit-faced on a regular basis?" he laughed.

Susan smiled. "Yes, more than that. For instance: loss of control. Once you take that first drink, if you cannot stop drinking until you pass out or black out and have no memory of the situation." She held up a finger with every new symptom.

"Undergoing a complete and almost immediate change in personality: like becoming angry and aggressive, or somber and depressive." She held two fingers in the air. "The craving phenomenon: when you go without alcohol and have overwhelming, unstoppable urges to drink." Now three fingers. "Increasing tolerance: when it takes more and more to satisfy your cravings." She held up four fingers. "When your life becomes unmanageable—if you lose your job or your friends, your material possessions or most importantly, your peace of mind. Those are the main ones." Five of her fingers were in the air. She put down her pen and crossed her hands in front of her.

"Alcohol affects an alcoholic on a cellular level in a different way than it does the non-alcoholic drinking population. I am going to write these things down and would like for you to take some serious time to consider them. Only you can determine if you have a drinking problem."

"I will," Thomas said nodding.

"Good. Now, I want to touch on something we've already discussed. You've said again that you don't feel like yourself, like you are someone else when you're out at the clubs at times. You have described another part of your personality, similar to Eagle, and I would like you to give him a name."

Thomas narrowed his eyes and thought about it. It made even more sense. "How about Big Mark? I like him because he is fearless and it makes it sound like he is one of the guys. I wish I could be him all the time."

"I understand how you feel Thomas, but it's important to understand that these 'fragments' of your personality were developed as part of your subconscious. We have yet to identify your true core self. I think your fragmented selves, no matter how much you like them, have some pretty bad habits that could be causing you the problems you are trying to resolve in your life. Does all this make any sense to you?"

"Yes, it really does."

"I don't want you to be discouraged Thomas. All the things you love about your fragmented personalities are already parts of your core self. They were each developed to serve purposes that are likely expired now. We will learn about this together and work together until you no longer need Eagle and Big Mark to protect you and give you confidence. I have faith in you and your strength and determination to be well and whole."

Thomas nodded. It all sounded so good. Everything Susan said to him gave him confidence and courage but today, he was antsy. He stood up to stretch his legs and wandered around the office. He stared out the window for a few minutes and then turned to look at the dozens of books that lined Susan's shelves.

"I see you glance at my books quite often. Do you like to read?" she asked him.

"Oh, yes. I read a lot. They remind me of my mother...your books."

"How so?"

"My mom used to read all the time. She never graduated high school and always regretted it so she started reading. She had so many books that one day I decided to build a wall of bookcases in our basement for her so she would have a place to put them. She gave me the money for the supplies, and I built them by hand, with a friend, from start to finish. Once they were done and the books were in place, I couldn't resist picking one up, and I was hooked."

Susan smiled.

"But now, I read mostly spiritual books or books about science. I was very religious growing up and studied the Bible a lot through various Christian faiths."

"Tell me about some of them," Susan said.

"Recently, I studied with a group of Jehovah's Witnesses." Thomas chuckled. "I met this really cute guy at the modeling agency. He was a body builder and you know, I fell in love with him like every other cute guy or girl I ever met who paid attention to me."

Susan smiled.

"He was openly gay, but he was seriously committed to his religion and fornication was forbidden. I knew I couldn't have sex with him, but I was in love with him, anyway. He asked me to accompany him to a Bible study, and I went. I wanted to be with him, and we often talked about religion together. I was intrigued."

"What did you get out of it?"

"Jehovah's Witnesses have a different way of looking at the Bible. They've researched word and language origin, and a few things made a tremendous difference in my life."

"Such as?"

"The word 'sin,' for one. Do you know that it originally means to simply 'miss the mark'? No punishment or guilt —if you were trying to go right and went left, you missed the mark. That freed me of so much guilt because that word, sin, had tormented me. I was obsessed with being a sinner and going to hell."

"Interesting."

"And 'hell' was another word that consumed my thoughts. The original word meant 'a shallow, open grave' and made no reference to a place of endless torment after death. I embraced this new knowledge. It spoke to my heart and my logic. It resonated inside me."

"How long did you study with them?" Susan asked.

"About nine months. But what they didn't realize," Thomas said laughing, "was that instead of embracing their dogma, which is their sole purpose on earth, it set me free!"

Susan laughed. "What else?"

"My last experience, other than reading countless New Age books, you know...*Ramtha, The White Book, Zen and the Art of Motorcycle Maintenance, Out on a Limb*...was dabbling in Buddhism. I would chant with a friend who introduced me to it but in the end, it all just became more dogma with new rules and regulations. I learned from every religion I have studied. My spiritual identity has evolved into something that's uniquely mine. God, just in case nobody ever told you Susan...is within."

"Do you still read the Bible?" Susan asked.

"No. I feel I have a deeper spiritual understanding now. "

Susan did not comment.

"Studying secular history along with current science and New Age theories has taught me more and spoken more to my heart. Science and my own spirit of reasoning have given me answers that the Bible, priests, and religion never have."

"I find your insight interesting, and I'm glad you shared it with me," she said. "As I said during our first session, anything you share with me will help us both in this process." She waited and looked at him expectantly, knowing that he had something else to share.

"Am I that transparent?" He sat down in one of the armchairs next to the couch.

Susan laughed. "Not at all. It's my job to know when my clients are troubled."

"Something else happened last night and I'm not proud of it."

"I never judge," Susan said. "And you haven't shocked me yet, Thomas."

They chuckled.

"There is this guy. I've seen him several times at my grocery store. He's really cute although not really my type. We finally said hello to one another the other day."

"Why do you say he isn't your type?"

"Well, he's tall and I prefer shorter guys. And he's as hairy as a beast and I do not like hairy guys! I know that sounds shallow, but I can't help what I'm attracted to."

Susan nodded. "I see. Why do you bring him up?"

"Because he happened to be out last night and I went home with him. We had sex and I was flipped out afterwards. When he got in the shower, I got dressed and left without saying a word."

Susan's face showed no emotion.

"I feel really bad about it, but I just couldn't deal with another one-night stand. My biggest reason for being here is to stop this pattern that I can't seem to break."

Susan crossed her arms. "Alright...so forgive yourself and move on. Clearly, the part of your personality that drinks too much is the same part that goes home with strangers. Identifying that is half the battle Thomas Paul. It might be a good exercise for you to contact him and apologize for leaving without a word."

"Oh, god. Are you kidding me?"

"I most certainly am not. It will release you from the guilt that you feel. More importantly, it will humanize this man. If you treat people with respect, as you hope to be treated, you are more likely to have purposeful experiences with them."

Thomas ruminated over her words.

"The damage may already be done with this guy, but you never know. If you see people as more human it may help you to avoid doing something with them that you will only regret later. Do you understand?"

He nodded. "Yes, I do and you're right. I will give it a shot."

"Does he have a name?" Susan asked.

"Yes. It's Daniel."

"I do hope you reach out to him. I'm sure it will make both you and Daniel feel better. Some people are good enough to meet our needs even when we think they may not be our type. If you humanize him, you never know, you might be surprised."

Chapter 22

Seventh Month of Therapy

"How was your week?" Susan asked.

"Uneventful for the most part, although you will be happy to know that I have been journaling." The small, black, leather-bound journal that Susan had given him months earlier, sat on his lap.

"Wonderful," Susan replied. "Glad to hear you are doing your homework."

"If it's okay, I'd like to read something to you."

"Of course, I'm all ears."

Thomas thumbed through the journal to the correct page and stared at it for a moment. He cleared his throat and started to read, his tone rhythmic and defiant. Susan watched Eagle emerge as the words he had written tumbled out and hung in the air.

"I was picked on, beat up, pushed around, and called names—made fun of, shouted at in the streets, spat on, hated, rejected and threatened within an inch of my life, my entire young life. All 'cause I look the way I look and act the way I act. For being gay.

It's hard not to hate back when you're hated. It's hard not to become a freak when you're treated like one. I don't know if I was born this way or not, but *however* it came to be, what does it really matter? My rights in my country are individual rights. I have the right to express myself freely. It was guaranteed me — same as everybody else. I didn't have to be born gay to be accepted for being gay. I am that I am!" Thomas closed the journal and waited.

Susan clapped her hands in approval. "That was wonderful. Do you mind if I ask what triggered that entry into your journal?"

Thomas thought for a moment. "I guess I just started thinking about when my family first became aware that I liked guys, not girls."

Susan nodded. "I've been wanting to delve into this and am glad to see that we are on the same page. So, when your family became aware, what was their reaction?"

"They weren't exactly thrilled."

"How old were you when you finally came out to them?"

"I was twenty-four but never really came out at all. I struggled with being gay and accepting myself for many years and that was difficult enough. I didn't believe I owed them an explanation." His voice was calm and matter-of-fact. "They were my family. I loved and accepted them, and I just assumed they felt the same way about me."

"Did you openly date men in front of them?" Susan asked.

"I would show up with guys but didn't offer any explanation that they were more than just friends. After a while, they put two and two together."

"And how did they react?"

"My younger sister confronted me one day, outraged and disgusted. She asked me if I was gay. The way she confronted me made me nervous." Thomas shook his head and frowned at the memory.

"I admitted it. She told me that I was an embarrassment to the family." His face darkened and he didn't speak for a moment. "She said my father was going to hit the roof and disown me when he found out—*Do you really expect us to all just accept this, Thomas Paul?* He mimicked her voice, complete with her sarcastic snort at the end.

This is something you are choosing. I don't understand it and I'm not sure if I can accept it. Don't think for one minute that my fiancé ever will. I'm afraid to tell him. He repeated her words verbatim. "Then she said that she didn't want to speak to me for a while, at least not until I had come to my senses."

"I see," Susan said. "And what did you do then?"

"I wrote a letter to my mother in retaliation. I told her that it was me who wanted nothing to do with them and that I didn't give a shit what they thought of me. That when I was ready, I would call them, not the other way around! I wrote that I had been treated horribly all of my life by strangers and acquaintances, and I wasn't about to tolerate being hated by them too. I owed them no explanation and they could all go to hell. If there was anyone to blame for me being gay it was them, and I was through being ashamed." His blood raced through his veins as he recalled the letter.

It had been a relief when he had written it years ago, and recounting it again was therapeutic. It steeled his confidence and his self-worth to proclaim the words out loud to Susan, and to himself. Susan crossed her arms and smiled at him with silent support.

Chapter 23

Twelfth Month of Therapy

As she always did during their sessions, Susan sat behind her large desk, pen poised on a legal pad, a warm smile on her face.

"Thomas. Do you know what sexualization is?"

"No, not really."

"To sexualize someone is, essentially, to make them sexual, or to make them aware of sexuality. But I'm not talking about your first consensual sexual experiences. People can be sexualized way before they choose to be sexual. Does this make sense to you?"

"Yes, I think so. Maybe...go on."

"Children are not born sexualized. And premature sexualization can have damaging, even devastating, effects on young children, which may continue on into adulthood if they aren't dealt with."

Thomas nodded his head, listening closely.

"Since you have come to me with specific concerns about relationships and intimacy, I think we should delve into this matter." Her voice was nurturing and calm. "Are you comfortable with this?"

"Absolutely. You're the doctor and I'm the patient." He smiled. Thomas was comfortable with Susan and felt safe in her office. He would tell her anything. He leaned back in the chair and reached deep into his memories. The therapy sessions with Susan were like remembering dreams, only it was his life replaying in his mind.

"Think back for me...what are some of your first sexual memories."

Thomas sat there in silence, with visions of the tee-pee, the wild boys, and the penis being shoved in his face still vivid after all these years. He recounted the story to Susan and watched for her reaction.

"So, you were not quite four years old?" Susan did not look up as she scribbled on her note pad.

Thomas nodded. "That's right."

"How does that make you feel today?"

"A little strange and confused, I guess."

Susan stopped writing and looked up. "Why?"

"'Cause after that day, I would sometimes get up at night when my brother was sleeping and look at him naked," he said.

"What did you feel when you looked at him?"

Thomas shrugged. "Scared...curious."

Susan flipped the page of the notepad and continued writing.

When she finally looked up at him, her expression was comforting and nonplussed. "It is a normal reaction — you were curious about him. However, what those kids were doing, although I'm sure they had no concept of it, was no less damaging. There were no parents or other responsible adults to guard you from things that were surely the result of at least one of those children having been exploited before."

Thomas was relieved.

"Did you have any other experiences like this at that age?"

"Not that I recall."

Susan was not ready to change the subject. "What about others? Were there any other sexual experiences that you can recall from your childhood? Things that you look back on now and feel different about."

Thomas drank from a water glass on the table in front of him; the ice inside it had melted, but it was still cool and refreshing.

"I don't know. I remember playing doctor with some of the kids in the neighborhood, mostly boys my own age."

Susan nodded as she scribbled.

"What else?" she asked.

"Well, there were girls, too. I had girlfriends," Thomas said.

Susan smiled. "I'm not surprised. Those blue eyes." She laughed. "Now, we are moving from sexualization to sexual experiences. Do you see the difference? Your girlfriends were of your choosing and they were your peers. The things you may have done together are different than if they had been done to you, by others."

"I get it." Thomas nodded.

"So, tell me about them, your peers."

"Well, my first real girlfriend was May. She was my sister's friend. She was sixteen and beautiful."

Susan's eyebrows shot up. "How old were you at the time?"

"I was twelve," Thomas said.

"Did anyone know about the relationship?"

"Oh, yeah. Everyone knew. I think my parents were just happy I was dating a girl."

Susan looked up from her notes. "So your parents were fine with the fact that you were only twelve to her sixteen?"

Thomas nodded. "Is that weird?"

"Well, it is a big age gap where teenagers are concerned. You were in middle school. May was a teenager in high school. Would they have let your sister date a sixteen-year-old boy when she was merely twelve?"

Thomas laughed. "When you put it that way, no. Absolutely not."

"Did you have sexual relations with May?" Susan asked.

"Well, we sure tried. But I was clueless about all of that. Same with Sally, my other girlfriend, and she was my age."

"When you look back on those relationships now, how do you feel?"

"I feel okay."

"Do you feel like continuing with this subject matter?"

"Sure. I'm fine."

"Good."

"Anyone or anything else you can think of?"

Thomas looked around the room and studied his surroundings. The wallpaper, the carpeting, Susan's framed diplomas, the shelves of books, the shiny philodendron plant in the corner — he felt more at home and comfortable in this room than he had in most any other room he had ever been in. He took a deep breath before speaking again.

"Well, I guess it was when I was at camp." He exhaled.

"The camp you went to as a young boy, Camp Evergreen?"

"Yes. But it was the first year I worked there. I was older."

Susan scribbled and waited. After a few moments of silence she spoke. "Are you sure you want to talk about it today? You seem hesitant."

Thomas swallowed a lump down his throat. "It's a little embarrassing. I haven't thought about it in a long time and didn't even realize it counted as a real sexual experience until now. I'm not proud of what I did. "

"I'm sure I won't be shocked, Thomas. But you don't have to tell me anything you don't want to."

"No, I want to tell you. Only one other person in the world knows about it."

Susan looked into his eyes and nodded. "It's okay."

Thomas felt heat rising to his face as he stared at the floor, studying the carpet pattern as he spoke. "There was this priest—he came to visit the camp and we became friends. When summer was over, he got in touch with me and we ended up having sex." Thomas did not look up as he continued talking. "I didn't like it very much and hated myself for doing it. He was a great guy and everybody liked him. I liked him, too, but I didn't like doing it with him. It only happened a few times and then I decided I didn't want to see him again."

Thomas wiped his brow and waited. Susan was silent. Her pen had stopped moving. For a moment, he worried that she would react as Sadie had years earlier.

Finally, she spoke again but did not resume writing. "How old were you when this first happened?

"Fifteen."

"How old was the priest, Thomas?"

"He was twenty-eight."

Thomas looked up from the floor and met her eyes. "Is something wrong, Susan?"

Her lip began to quiver and did not stop as she spoke. "Do you know that what he did to you was wrong, Thomas Paul?"

What he did to you? "What do you mean what he did to me? No! It was me — wasn't it?"

He cocked his head to the side with a dumbfounded look of disbelief. A well of emotions churned and stewed inside of him. *What he did to you?*

His weary burden from years of deep self-loathing, denial, and self-imposed blame shifted slightly. Realizing that he may have been the victim and not the one at fault stupefied him. What *he* did to *you*?

Susan's face was awash with love, compassion, and understanding as she listened to him un-burden his heavy load. Thomas broke down in uncontrollable sobs, his body shaking with spasms from the entire spectrum of emotions he was experiencing. He went on to tell what he had never told anyone and confessed to her in great detail all that the priest had done to him.

From behind her desk, Susan remained professional. She kept her distance, offering him tissues and silent support as she wept quietly along with him.

Chapter 24

The Following Session

"There are a lot of adult survivors of child sexual abuse who find healing in confronting their perpetrators. It can be an empowering experience for the victims, provide them with closure, and bring accountability to the offenders. You have a unique opportunity to do something that not all people do because you know your perpetrator's identity and how to locate him."

Susan paused, looked at Thomas, and waited for him to comment.

"Are you suggesting that's something I should do?"

"It's entirely your decision. As your therapist, it is my job to provide you with facts and information concerning this issue."

Thomas thought to himself for a moment. "If I decided I wanted to do something like that, how on earth would I go about it?"

"You could approach the church on your own, or you could ask someone to be your mediator," Susan replied.

"Oh, I think I get it," Thomas smirked. "Could that someone be you?"

"Yes, it could be, if you asked me."

"If I confronted him, do you think I could force the church to make sure he never hurt anyone again?"

"I like the way you think. Yes, if that is what you want you can approach him through a representative of the church who will have the authority to make decisions like that."

Thomas was getting comfortable with the idea. "Will you help me do this?"

Susan grinned. "I most certainly will."

After a moment of silence came the mutual realization of a newly formed alliance between them.

"There is one more thing. Once a victim has confronted a perpetrator, he or she has a one-year statute of limitations to bring a legal claim to sue for damages. After that year is up, no claim can be made."

Thomas shook his head. "I'm a hair-stylist, Susan. It's 1989. Despite the research, people think they'll contract AIDS if some gay guy simply sneezes on them. Most of my clientele don't know I'm gay. You know how narrow-minded this town is. If I sue and press charges, it will be public, and I could be ruined. My career is the first thing I've ever done on my own and I'm damn good at it. I don't want to risk losing it and this is not about money, anyway it's about justice. I don't think I want to sue, but I am certain about one thing: I know now that I want to confront him."

"Then by all means, Thomas, you have my unyielding support."

*   *   *

Thomas sat on the couch, smoking a cigarette, while Susan busied herself rearranging the office furniture to insure that the priests would be seated across the room from them. Her voice was nurturing and reassuring as she explained how the confrontation would unfold.

"I'm proud of you, Thomas, and soon you will see that confronting Stumpf will play a big part in your healing. How do you feel?"

"I'm okay. I just want this over with so I never have to see him again." It was partly true. He had accepted the importance of a single face-to-face meeting with Stumpf and was somewhat relieved at the thought of possibly putting his pain behind him once and for all. But he wasn't as okay as he seemed. Inside he was scared to death and filled with uncertainty and loathing at the idea of seeing the priest again. He wanted to suck down the whole pack of cigarettes in his pocket, one after the other, until his lungs were dry and his nerves were numb.

"Indeed," Susan said.

Reverend Hampton, director of the Church's charity division, wore his official garb as opposed to Reverend Stumpf, who had donned a layman's suit for the meeting. Thomas Paul's pulse quickened as he watched them enter the office and seat themselves in the strategically placed chairs across the room. Stumpf kept his eyes trained on the ground and appeared nervous, a stark contrast to the confidence and swagger he displayed all those years ago at camp. He had put on some weight and even clothed, appeared soft and doughy. His skin was pale and ghostlike, making his hairiness appear more pronounced—except for the hair on his head, which had thinned with the years. Thomas couldn't believe that the man had ever not repulsed him. The fact that this person had once been like a shiny, magnetic beacon to any and all he ever encountered was almost incomprehensible. He wondered what the priest was thinking and took comfort, even pleasure, in the stark shift in power between them.

Thomas was present in his adult self, better able to manage the strong-willed fragments of the personalities he had named and come to understand. He was in control of them today, like a loving parent, just as Susan had taught him to be.

After introductions, Susan turned to Thomas and spoke. "So that all is clear for everyone present, Thomas, the sole purpose of this confrontation is to empower you. If at any time you wish to speak, please feel free to do so, and if you need a break, just stand up and exit the room and I will follow you. Also, as we've already agreed, Mr. Stanton will not be pressing criminal charges against Mr. Stumpf and has no intention to sue for damages. However, the Church has promised to reimburse Mr. Stanton for all past therapy sessions and continue to pay for any ongoing therapy, as long as it is deemed necessary. Finally, Mr. Stumpf is to be removed from his position as director of the troubled-youth program at Serenity hospital, prevented from holding any future clerical positions involving children, and placed in intensive therapy."

She turned to Reverend Hampton. "Is this still our understanding?"

"Yes."

"Fine, then. I have explained to Mr. Stanton that your representative, Father Stumpf, has freely and openly confessed to all accusations made against him by my client. Those include childhood molestation, including oral and anal sex, and providing a minor with alcohol and drugs. It is my understanding, Reverend Hampton, that this admission was made in front of the Archbishop, with his full understanding and awareness of the things I've just mentioned."

Reverend Hampton nodded. "Yes, indeed it was. His Holiness is fully aware of Father Stumpf's admission of the acts he committed against Mr. Stanton while Mr. Stanton was a minor."

"Reverend Hampton, would you please speak directly to my client and repeat what you've just said," Susan asked.

The priest cleared his throat and did as he was asked.

Susan turned to Thomas. "Thomas Paul, is there anything you would like to say? Take as much time as you need, and if you feel the need to take a moment in the other room first, please do so."

Thomas stared at the floor for a long time and fought the impulse to light another cigarette. Finally, he looked at Stumpf, and Little Thomas spoke.

"You could have been our hero and saved us, but you didn't."

The room was silent, the air thick with apprehension. Father Stumpf raised his head and waited.

Thomas, the man, looked directly into his perpetrator's eyes. His voice was firm and angry, yet restrained.

"You ruined my life."

The simple yet heavy words hung in the air. "I have had to fight like an animal to get it back and ultimately, I know that I have to forgive you. So, I will do just that. I forgive you. And I want you to know that *I* will go on to become ten times the man you are but *your* salvation, Father Bob, is between you and God."

Stumpf's eyes focused downward once again.

Susan placed her hand on Thomas' shoulder and whispered, "I'm proud of you. You're a very brave man."

Thomas reached up and squeezed her hand.

"If Mr. Stumpf has anything to respond, will you allow it?" she asked.

Thomas nodded.

"Mr. Stumpf, would you care to say anything to Mr. Stanton?" Susan asked.

Stumpf's voice, though barely audible, was that of a broken and defeated man.

"I'm sorry that I caused you so much pain and anguish."

The room remained silent for a moment. Reverend Hampton and Susan stood and exchanged a few words, and the priests exited the office.

"How do feel now?" Susan asked, once they were alone. Thomas embraced her and held her for a longwhile."

Thank you," he whispered to her.

Susan was right. The freedom he felt astonished him. It felt like a weight had been lifted from him. The reality of what the priest had done to him had been choking his spirit for years. Dark and fetid, it lurked in the depths of his mind and deep in his heart and soul, preventing any goodness from taking a permanent hold in his life. The priest's admission and apology had cemented in Thomas Paul's mind what Susan had tried to help him recognize, through endless hours of therapy — that he was not to blame for what happened. He could already feel something new inside—hope. The shackles of self-doubt began to lift and float away from him like feathers in the wind. He felt free.

Chapter 25

Thirtieth Month of Therapy

"How are you today?" Susan asked.

"I'm doing well. Really well, in fact," Thomas answered.

"I can tell. You've come so far since our first meeting. I'm proud of your progress, Thomas."

"It's thanks to you, Susan. I didn't think the clouds would ever permanently lift for me. But I do believe they are starting to and will only continue to do so."

Susan nodded. "I appreciate your compliment but remember, I have only been your guide. You have done the heavy lifting." She smiled and continued. "Half of what we get out of life depends on just showing up for it, Thomas. You sought me out and showed up week after week for our sessions. You did the exercises I suggested—from soul searching to journaling, to naming your alter egos. By doing all that, you have begun to heal yourself. You have re-engaged in life.

Thomas nodded as she spoke.

"Today is a big day. I have two important things I want to discuss with you," she said.

"Hmmm, should I be worried?"

"Not at all," she reassured him. "First of all, I believe we have worked together long enough and that I have gathered sufficient information to give you my diagnosis. Do you feel ready for that?"

"Absolutely."

"It is my belief that you suffer, and have suffered for a long time, from complex-post traumatic stress disorder."

Thomas Paul's eyes widened. "Well, that sure is a mouth full."

"Indeed it is. C-PTSD, as it's known, is a psychological injury resulting from prolonged exposure to trauma, usually during childhood, when there is no way for the victim to escape. The trauma can, and most certainly does in your case, include physical, mental, sexual, and emotional abuse. Oftentimes, the effects and symptoms of childhood C-PTSD don't fully present until adulthood."

Thomas listened, a slight furrow in his brow.

"Just because you displayed certain effects from the disorder in your young adulthood doesn't mean you didn't have symptoms as a young child. C-PTSD has a considerable morbidity rate, particularly for children. Your victimization lasted as long as any other person had power over you and caused you serious harm. The traumatic events in your life—the teepee as a young child, your father's beatings, your mother's illness, the bullying, and the abuse at the hands of the priest, sent you down a volatile developmental path."

Thomas sat motionless, still silent, drinking in her words.

"There are a host of emotional and behavioral problems that can arise as a result of the disorder, and you have suffered from several throughout your life. Your constant headaches and stomachaches as a child, your hyper-arousal, your depression—which caused your persistent thoughts of death and suicide—your inability to concentrate and participate in normal academic and social activities, your dissociated personalities, your constant fight-or-flight response to stress and your anxiety were symptoms. These are all effects from C-PTSD."

Thomas was intrigued that his problems actually had a name. A serious-sounding name. "All those things are the result of being abused? So I wasn't crazy?"

Susan smiled. "Of course not. And yes, abused children, particularly children who are physically and sexually abused repeatedly, suffer significantly high rates of C-PTSD." She continued. "And once you entered adulthood and tried to have normal adult relationships, you became aware that something was wrong."

"Will I get better? Will I need medication?" It had always been his fear that he would follow in the footsteps of his mother and end up spiraling down into the abyss of drug addiction and despair.

"Don't you see, Thomas, you are getting better. There is no magic pill for the primary diagnosis of C-PTSD. There is a barrage of medicines that are sometimes used to treat the effects. You've done so well without medication that I believe you may never need it at this point. You've been so highly motivated, and through the cognitive-behavioral therapy work we have done so far, you have unlearned much of your learned behavior.

"Learned behavior can be unlearned. You've replaced many of your negative feelings with positive ones. That is how it works. There are no magic formulas or cures for many psychological disorders. One just has to make a determined effort to change his or her behavior and get on a new, better life path."

Thomas nodded. "You know, now that we're talking about it, I have to admit that I have been in a good place lately."

"It should only get better, if you continue to work at it. CBT has a beginning and an end, and you and I will not need to see each other forever."

"I do know that. I know it has always been our goal for me not to need therapy one day, but I don't much like the idea of not seeing you anymore."

"I take that as another compliment and this brings me to the other important thing I wanted to discuss with you. I've taken a new job, in another city." She waited for his reaction.

Thomas stared at her with a look of surprise on his face.

"I know it seems sudden but I have been given an opportunity that I can't pass up, and I want you to know that I waited until I thought you were ready before I accepted it. I won't be leaving for another six months, so I have ample time to phase-out with my patients. I care very much about you and your prognosis. You were my friend before you were my patient. I wouldn't dream of leaving if I didn't firmly believe you were strong enough to continue on with your healing, possibly with another therapist but mainly on your own."

"A new therapist?"

"Once I leave, I think it would be a good idea for you to transition out of therapy with another therapist who also offers group sessions. I have some names to give you."

Thomas didn't know how to feel. He was upset that she was leaving but he knew she was right; he had the tools to continue his healing on his own. It was time to spread his wings and stop relying on her. He was ready. He couldn't begrudge her any future success; she had helped save him. He only wanted the best for her.

"Will they be as good as you?" he asked.

"They come very highly recommended but, truth be told, at this point in time, I think you may benefit more from group therapy than one-on-one sessions. Thomas, I think you have much to share with others. I think your story and your progress could help a lot of people. I believe in you, in your strength, and in your heart. In helping others, we help ourselves."

"Do you really think I'm strong enough?"

"I knew right away when we started our sessions that you were going to be okay." She smiled. "There's an old saying that reminds me of you… *the cream always rises to the top.*"

Thomas smiled back at her. "Thank you for that," he said, encouraged by her words. "Before we finish, can I ask you a question?"

"Certainly."

"After everything we've gone over today, it's made me think of something—something I've wondered about for a while."

"What is it?"

"Do you think that everything I went through as a kid could have made me gay?"

Susan tilted her head at the question and shrugged. "Who's to say, Thomas? Plenty of people went through what you did and more and did not become gay. As well, plenty of people are gay but never went through anything like you did. Do you think what you went through made you gay?"

"I don't know, Susan. I suppose it's possible but… I really don't think so."

Chapter 26

Thomas pushed his shopping cart through the grocery store and headed for the produce section. He had become obsessed with Julia Child and was developing into quite a skilled chef under her tutelage on television and from pouring over her favorite cookbook, *From Julia Child's Kitchen*. He picked up a tomato and squeezed it. Just then, he felt someone watching him. He knew who it was without even having to spot him. *Oh my God, are you kidding me?* He thought to himself. He felt the color rise to his face. *He's human.* Susan's words played over in his mind.

Thomas took a deep breath, looked up, met Daniel's gaze and smiled. Much to his relief, Daniel smiled back and wandered over to him.

"Umm....do we know each other?" Daniel teased.

Thomas smiled and held up his hand. "Daniel, I'm sorry for being a dick. I shouldn't have run out on you. It was really shitty of me."

Daniel smiled. "I appreciate that. So, how have you been?"

They chatted for a moment until the tension had disappeared.

"I'd like to see you again. Would you like to come over for dinner?" Daniel asked.

Give him a chance; he might surprise you. Again, Susan counseled him from the back of his mind.

"I would like that very much. Let me make it up to you— I'll cook."

"That sounds great," Daniel said.

"On one condition, though. I'm renovating my house and it's a disaster. How about I bring the food to your place?"

That had been months earlier, and now Thomas stood back for a moment and watched as Daniel made final adjustments on a door to a closet they had built together. Susan had been right, as usual, and Daniel had become an integral part of his life. They had taken things slowly, and it was becoming the first real relationship that Thomas had ever had. Not only had Daniel turned out to be supportive and kind, he was handy and talented and was an immense help to Thomas as he renovated his home.

The purchase and renovation of this house was like a second form of therapy for Thomas. Just as he was re-designing and renovating this old house, he was doing the same to his mind, heart, and soul — fixing them.

Thomas would find that throughout his life, his emotional journeys and life changes and growths would often coincide with the re-designing and renovating of homes. The projects would play an important part in the re-birth of the artist within him, helping to nurture the creativity and artistic expression that had been stifled and distorted as a child.

*   *   *

Thomas leaned up against the bar to keep from swaying. He'd consumed several drinks and watched the crowd gyrate on the dance floor.

"Hey, Tommy!"

Thomas turned around at the sound of the bartender, a friend of his, calling his name.

"What's up, Todd?"

"Hey, I thought you got that priest kicked out?"

"What do you mean?" Thomas was on edge at the mention of the word priest.

"I work at Serenity Hospital during the day, remember? It's Stumpf, right? The one who runs the troubled-youth program? He's still there. I just thought you should know."

Thomas Paul's mind raced and the news sobered him up. "Are you sure?"

"Positive. I saw him there with my own eyes just yesterday."

Thomas took a moment to gather his senses. Still emotionally charged from the alcohol, he started crying and bolted for the club exit. He raced to Daniel's house, not far from his own, and pounded on the front door. Moments later, Daniel answered.

Thomas pushed his way inside, hysterical.

"What's going on?" Daniel was panicked at Thomas Paul's frenzy.

"The priest is still there!"

"Where, Thomas? Where?"

"Still in charge of all those kids at the hospital. Todd told me, at the club tonight."

"Okay, calm down."

"I won't fucking calm down! I did it for nothing. I confronted him for nothing. They promised me — they lied to me. They fucked me over again!" Thomas paced back and forth, alternating between fits of anger and uncontrollable tears.

"I don't know what to do. I've got to do something!"

"Okay. We'll figure it out," Daniel tried to calm him, handing him tissues and holding him.

Finally, after hours of distress and trying to comfort him, Daniel, now emotional and upset, offered, "I don't know what else to do for you, Thomas. Maybe I should call Susan." He reached for the phone and dialed, praying that she would answer at such a late hour.

Thomas did not protest. Later, after a lengthy conversation with Susan, he was able to calm down. She convinced him that there was nothing they could do until the next day. He collapsed in bed.

Thomas struggled for days trying to decide how to proceed. The implications of this newfound information overwhelmed him. It had been almost a year since his confrontation with Stumpf, and obviously Hampton and the church had slipped into complacency regarding their promises.

Thomas paced the floor again while Daniel, now a great source of strength and support, watched with worry.

"I know of at least one other guy," Thomas said, "a friend of Todd's, who was molested by Stumpf, as well. If there were two of us, there are bound to be more. Why would he stop now if no one is watching over him? They've only slapped him on the wrist. I have to do something."

"I think you're right. You should do something, but what? Are you sure you can handle laying yourself bare again after all this time has passed? It breaks my heart to see you so distressed."

"I made a promise to Hampton that I had no intention of taking further action as long as they made sure Stumpf was dealt with as agreed. In spite of my father being as horrible as he was, he did teach me to be a man of my word. Even though it pains me to go back on it, they are the ones who fucked it all up. I had closure, and they've taken it away. If I go to them and ask them to honor their word to me, why the hell would they now if they haven't already? With no threat of exposure from publicity or no financial burden imposed upon them, what is their motivation to honor those promises? I need to get their attention."

Daniel nodded. "Whatever you decide to do, I hope it will bring you closure and peace of mind once and for all, not just more stress and anguish."

Thomas sat down at his desk and started writing.

Late into the night, after several drafts and re-writes, he finally put down his pen.

"I've written a letter. It's only part of what I plan to do, but read it and tell me what you think." He handed the papers to Daniel.

Daniel read in wide-eyed silence. "Are you sure you want to do this?"

"I'm scared to death but yes, it's what I have to do."

"I love you and if you really feel you need to do this, you have my support. But Susan isn't here, Thomas. Do you think you can handle this on your own?"

"As long as you stand by me, I'll be okay."

"What about your statute of limitations? Do you think you will get this together before it expires?"

"I don't intend to. First things first, though. A simple phone call should be sufficient for getting the priest out. Then I will decide what to do with the letter."

The following day, despite the gnawing angst in the pit of his stomach, Thomas called Reverend Hampton. With a strong and sure voice, he informed him that he was prepared to go to the newspapers and the news media if the church did not keep its original part of the agreement and remove Stumpf immediately. He warned them that this time he would see to it that they kept their word.

But his threats went unheeded. Months of similar phone calls fell on deaf ears, and Thomas Paul decided there was only one thing left to do. He mailed the letter.

Chapter 27

Three Months Later

Thomas sat in a conference room of the office tower and watched as heavy rain ran down the massive windows. Thunder rattled the immense glass panes that walled the room. He loved thunderstorms, and this one calmed him as he sat alone, waiting, in the large institutional room. The space was sparse except for a long, gleaming, green marble table and surrounding dark brown, plush leather chairs.

So this was the church's attorney's office, he thought to himself. Thomas had been surprised to learn that the church had its own lawyers. He wondered if the receptionist who showed him to the boardroom knew why he was there. She seemed pleasant enough and even smiled as she offered him a beverage.

Lightning lit up the sky and for a brief second, he mused that God himself was trying to intimidate him.

Finally, the door to the conference room opened and a line of people trailed in, seating themselves in a row on the opposite side of the table from Thomas. Reverend Hampton, the church spokesman, sat at the head of the table and introduced two attorneys—another priest, who was a representative for the church—and a secretary. Thomas remained seated, his hands folded on the table. He showed no emotion. The truth held him steady.

"While we all know the nature of our meeting today, Thomas—" one of the attorneys, Mr. Compton, said.

"Excuse me," Thomas interrupted, "but I would prefer it if you call me Mr. Stanton."

The attorney nodded. "Very well, Mr. Stanton. I will continue and say again that while we know why we are here, for the sake of the record I am going to have Ms. Pearce, as long as you approve, read the letter you have given to Reverend Hampton." Thomas nodded his approval.

Ms. Pearce cleared her throat and began to read.

> *Dear Father Hampton,*
>
> *I, Thomas Paul Stanton, am seeking financial security as compensation for the pain and suffering and also for the emotional and psychological damage inflicted upon me since my fifteenth year, as a direct result of the slow, calculated corruption, through manipulation and seduction, forced upon me by Reverend Robert Stumpf, a representative of the Catholic Church.*
>
> *Restitution is sought in the form of a gift, paid to me by the Church, in the amount of $500,000.*
>
> *The gift will stand as testimony from the Church that the losses sustained during the last fifteen years of my life are held valuable and worthwhile by*

the Church and that the Church is taking responsibility for those losses.

The gift also insures the financial security needed to maintain my present level of income so that I may more diligently pursue my emotional and psychological recovery, through intensive in-patient or out-patient therapy, without any worry of the serious and critical long-term damage this pursuit may potentially cause to my career.

This is the most expeditious, least costly, and least publicized settlement the Church can make to bear the responsibility for my recovery from the actions taken against me as a youth.

If restitution cannot be made, then I will seek other avenues available to me, which will not be beneficial to either the Church or me.

Thank you.
Thomas Paul Stanton.

Thomas felt proud listening to someone else read his letter aloud. He had composed it and had presented it to the church all on his own, with no representation. He felt empowered. He had purposely let the statute of limitations expire. To continue his healing and his journey to live a structured, stable life, he wanted the Church, *without threat of suit*, to humbly and willingly acknowledge the harm caused to him at their hands and validate his worthiness and value as a human being.

Reverend Jenkins spoke. "I wanted to speak first, Mr. Stanton. This must seem pretty intimidating to you but let me assure you, that is not our intention. Apparently you have been through a lot and none of us want to put you through any more, but, considering what you are asking, it is essential that we fully understand the justification for such a measure."

Thomas stared at him.

"I am here to make an evaluation to present to Archbishop Murray, who was disheartened when Reverend Hampton informed him that you refused his request to be present at this meeting. May I ask why you did not want the archbishop to be present for this meeting?"

"No," Thomas replied. He would not tell them that he would have been far too intimidated to have the Archbishop present. Even though Thomas was far from practicing anymore, being raised Catholic had cemented within him, the powers, real or not, of such a looming figure of authority.

"Very well, Mr. Stanton. The archbishop doesn't get turned down very often and it was simply a matter of curiosity." He chuckled, trying to lighten the mood. "You gave Reverend Hampton your permission to share with those of us here today what he knows about this case."

Thomas interrupted. "That's correct, but it's not a case. I have no legal rights here. We all know it. This is what happened to me, my story—my life. Please don't refer to it as a case."

The Reverend continued. "May we call them your experiences, then—so that we may have a point of reference?"

"Yes."

"Will it be alright if I go over some facts and ask you a few questions before Mr. Compton takes over? Please understand that you are in no way obligated to answer anything that you do not wish to answer, but the more information I have to present to the Archbishop, the better we will be able to decide what should be done in your favor."

"That's fine."

The Reverend nodded and glanced at some notes he had placed on the table in front of him. "You have been in therapy for over three years now. We know the general history of your experiences with Reverend Stumpf and of the confrontation with him last year, including his full admission to the accusations of molestation. As well, we have read your letter. To reassure you, Mr. Stanton there has been no disclosure of the exact details of those experiences. Only the nature of the violation in general terms. Since you were not seeking legal restitution it was considered unnecessary to press you for any painful issues."

"At the time, you made it clear that it was not your intention to press criminal charges or to sue the Church. I believe you said that your only interest was to see to it that," he began to read verbatim from his notes, "the Church assume responsibility for Reverend Stumpf and keep a watchful eye over him so that he could no longer offend anyone else. Is that close to what you said?"

"Yes, it is. If the church excommunicated him, who would watch over him? If he were convicted he would only serve a short time in jail, get out embittered and, without the watchful eye of the Church, position himself to hurt others again. And take my word for it, he would know exactly how to go about doing that if he chose to. All the therapy in the world would not erase that knowledge for him," Thomas said.

"Did the Church not do as you asked, Mr. Stanton? It is my understanding that Reverend Stumpf was removed from his parish and was assigned, with his consent, to a long-term treatment center. He is also to attend weekly therapy sessions for the rest of his life. Eventually he will be made co-pastor, under a pastor who is fully aware of his story, at a church well removed from children. Finally, that he would never again be involved in any youth programs. Those things did indeed happen as you requested." The Reverend, a quizzical look upon his face, looked up at Thomas.

Thomas cleared his throat. "Those things did happen, Reverend Jenkins. However, I was promised that they would happen immediately after our confrontation and his admission of wrongdoing. Obviously, Reverend Hampton did not fill you in on the whole truth. I trusted the Church to do what they promised and went on with my life. Nearly a year later it was made known to me by a friend who worked at Serenity Hospital, that Reverend Stumpf had never been removed from his position of director of the troubled-youth program there. The Church lied to me. I called Reverend Hampton and confronted him."

"I was aware of the issue, Mr. Stanton and humbly apologize. It can take time to bring about changes of that nature."

Thomas felt his mouth go dry. *That's just what any abuse victim wants to hear, just give us more time and we'll make it stop. Just hold on a little while longer.*

It was all he could do to hold his tongue.

Reverend Jenkins continued speaking under the weight of Thomas Paul's stare. "I believe it was all explained to you at the time you came to Reverend Hampton, and that the changes were indeed put into place. Has it been to your satisfaction?

Thomas was slow to reply. "Yes."

"Archbishop Murray wanted me to sincerely apologize for your suffering and to extend to you his deepest sympathy. He also wants to extend to you an open invitation to contact him at any point in the future should you change your mind about meeting him. He is a very caring person and only wishes for your well-being." The Reverend waited for a response from Thomas but was greeted with silence.

With crimson cheeks, he went on. "Finally, Mr. Stanton, Archbishop Murray would like you to give serious consideration to returning to the loving arms of the Church in hopes that it may help you find peace in the Lord through its kinship." He paused once more. "I have said all that is needed and will now turn the rest of our meeting over to Mr. Compton, who will be asking you some detailed questions. I urge you to answer willingly and openly so that, under these new circumstances, we may more fully understand the nature of your experiences with Reverend Stumpf."

The room was hushed for several minutes as the two attorneys conversed. Finally, Mr. Compton turned to Thomas.

"How are you doing in therapy, Mr. Stanton?"

"I am doing well, thank you. I'm determined, a fighter and a survivor. Although at times it seems I still have a long way to go. I want to lose that language that describes victims. I don't want to be labeled a survivor forever. I want to be a whole functioning person—survivors are often still broken. I don't want to be broken anymore," Thomas said.

Mr. Compton smiled and nodded. "I understand that after the initial confrontation, the Church agreed to pay for your ongoing therapy until such time that you and your therapist deemed it no longer necessary. As well, you have been reimbursed for all your sessions prior to the confrontation."

Thomas nodded.

"In your letter to Reverend Hampton you stated that you might need to pursue more intensive therapy. What kind of therapy might you be referring to?"

"In general, Mr. Compton, more sessions require more time hence, interfering with work. As for anything specific, that is not a question I care to answer at the risk of re-victimizing myself here in this office. But if you insist it is absolutely necessary, I will discuss it with my therapist and possibly try to explain it."

"We don't want to invade your privacy, but the purpose for my question is to try and determine a dollar value to place on this. The Church has informed me that they can't justify such an exorbitant amount of money and that without serious justification for it, some kind of compromise will have to be made." He looked at Thomas.

Thomas Paul stared back at him, again without emotion.

The attorney continued. "For now, we'll move on. Since you are doing so well in therapy and the Church is willing to continue paying for it, could you explain further why you are asking for this large sum of money?"

Thomas sat in his chair like his father had taught him, shoulders back, head raised, eyes straight ahead, and looked the attorney square in the eye. He searched his heart for the words and for the first time in his life, he spoke for himself with unwavering courage. "Because it is the only thing they can do, Mr. Compton. The only thing that would even come close to matching the value of what I have lost at their hands— financial security. They most certainly can, and they should. They should feel at least a sliver of the burden that I, and likely many others, have carried. They can't give me back my innocence or my dignity. They can't reproduce for me all the unrealized opportunities lost from the years of shame tattooed on my person. Shame I wore daily for all the world to see. I lost my opportunity for education due to my mental obsession over that shame. *I blamed myself.* I was a horrible student and barely graduated high school. I alienated any hopes of friends because of my feelings of unworthiness and self-loathing. I may potentially struggle for a lifetime to undo the damage inflicted upon me." Thomas paused and looked at each person sitting across from him.

"That priest could have been my savior. I needed him to be just that and instead—he ruined me. And they knew. They *all* knew. Not a single other clergy person in that house ever spoke up and said stop. *Stop what you are doing to that boy.*" Thomas Paul's voice was steady and strong. He looked back at Mr. Compton. "He exploited me, and the Church should give me this gift uncompromised, as there was no compromise in the level of corruption imposed upon me."

The room was silent until Mr. Compton spoke again. "Tell us in great detail, Mr. Stanton, of all your experiences with Reverend Stumpf—from beginning to end, please."

Thomas was shocked. It had never occurred to him that he would have to talk to this group of authority figures about such sensitive, private things. He had gone from confident to vulnerable in one fell swoop, and it was clear that to get what he wanted and deserved, he would have to divulge everything. After years of therapy with Susan, he was aware that his other personalities were at the ready, waiting to help him endure the humiliation that he would feel from this confession.

Little Thomas spoke first with the innocence of a young child, recounting the encounters with Father Bob at camp and elsewhere. He spoke plainly, without fear or embarrassment. But soon, Eagle broke through, agitated at having to remember the shame he still felt from what had happened years ago and again now from having to tell it to all these strangers. Conspirators. His voice was heavy with sarcasm as he drilled his eyes into Mr. Compton's own. "He groomed us to do his bidding, the filthy son-of-a-bitch! He got us to open our mouth for him so he could push his fucking dick in it and spit his wad down our throat! Part of it in our mouth and part of it down our throat, making us gag and choke, with the rest of it dripping down our chin — you bunch of fuckers."

Eagle was yelling now but kept on. "We walked to the garbage can to spit it out; gagging, trying not to look like it bothered us so we wouldn't seem uncool—and the pig just laid there, still hard, and watched us. He believed we did it because we liked it and then pretended to care and ask us 'is everything okay with you?'"

Eagle recounted every detail of the corruption at the hands of the priest. Once again, the room was silent.

Eagle paused and again made eye contact with the attorney. "Has anybody ever done that to you when you were a kid, Mr. Lawyer? How about your kids? You care if somebody ever does that to your kids, Mr. Lawyer? What do *you* think it would be worth if they did?" Thomas Paul was crying now and stopped talking when he realized where he was. He cast his eyes downward to regain his composure but not before seeing that his loss of control had left every person at the table in shock and staring at him, agog.

"No, it was not done to me, Mr. Stanton. Nor would I want it to happen to my children or anyone else's children for that matter. Thank you for being so honest. Is there more that you would like to say?"

Thomas nodded and sniffled. "My challenge is one I am not sure you can relate to. I don't want to live a life struggling with bitterness, resentment, and self-loathing. To do that I need two things. One being this gift from the Church and the other is to be able to forgive. My parents and yes, the Church, taught me that. I needed to forgive him—my perpetrator. I had to be the kind of person I was taught to be but so rarely see in my day-to-day existence. I told Reverend Stumpf to his face that I forgave him, and I did it so that I could be free. It was the longest journey I have ever taken to date, Mr. Compton, the distance from my head to my heart." With that Thomas had said all he could.

There was another moment of silence and some quiet paper-shuffling. "It seems we have what we need, Mr. Stanton."

Thomas nodded.

"One final question, though, if you don't mind. What are 'the other avenues available to you that you mention in your letter?"

Thomas was candid. "Although I have no interest in making my story public, I do intend to pursue it if the Church won't agree to my offer. This will be a critical part of my recovery, and it's more than the money. It's about the Church's willingness to give freely, without threat, as a testament that they deem my life valuable. However, if they cannot sum up that level of generosity and charity, I'm quite sure Oprah Winfrey, Phil Donahue or some publishing company would do so, to help me further my healing."

Mr. Compton pursed his lips together and nodded slowly.

"I don't mean that as a threat. It's simply what I would do," Thomas said.

Chapter 28

After confronting Stumpf, and finally meeting with the attorneys and representatives from the Church, Thomas decided that it was time to tell his mother about everything. He had never breathed a word about anything having to do with Stumpf to anyone in his family, but he couldn't keep it a secret any longer. His mother would then tell his father, as that was how it worked in the Stanton family. All things passed through their mother first, and being keenly aware of her husband's intolerance with most things to do with their children, she would then pass on a filtered version of all events to him and try to avoid setting off his short temper.

"Your mother told me what happened between you and that priest you used to hang out with, Thomas Paul," his father said to him. "That son-of-a-bitch would have gotten a few things from me, including my fucking fist down his throat if I had known that he was doing things like that to any son of mine, goddamnit! You know that, don't you, son? That I would have stood up for you?"

Thomas Paul swallowed a lump down his throat but before he could speak, his mother chimed in.

"That wouldn't have done any good, Johnny! Back then they would have locked you up for assaulting a priest and then what would we have done? You would have been in jail and there would have been no one to take care of me. I couldn't have handled any trouble like that." She looked over at her son and back to her husband. "Besides, Thomas Paul is *fine*. They are going to compensate him well and everything will stay peaceful." She collapsed into a chair, frail and out of breath but satisfied that she had smoothed things over.

His father spoke again. "Your mother also told me that you're trying to get money from them?"

Thomas nodded but said nothing.

"I guess I don't blame you son, but goddamnit, Thomas Paul, it will just come out of my ass one way or another. Looks like my weekly Sunday contribution in the church's collection basket is gonna go up, and I can guaran-goddamn-tee-ya that is where the money they pay you is gonna come from." He ended his sentence with a boisterous guffaw.

Thomas stayed silent. He would never, ever mention the matter again with anyone in his family.

Months later, Thomas spent a strained but enlightening Christmas with his family—seeing them more clearly. He loved them but did not respect them. He couldn't relate to them as parents and could not figure out how to fit them into his life. He realized that if they had not been related by blood, he would never befriend them. He left the house that evening without a word and distanced himself without explaining anything to anyone. He would not pacify them any longer. It was late January 1992. He received a call from the Church. This time, Thomas was shown to a different office and was not kept waiting. Mr. Compton, the church's attorney, was seated at his desk, waiting for him. He looked up at the sound of his secretary knocking on his open door, stood, and offered his hand to Thomas.

"Good afternoon, Mr. Stanton."

Thomas shook his hand.

"Obviously, the circumstances are quite different from the last time you were here."

Thomas nodded. "They sure are. I'm glad it's almost over."

Mr. Compton sat back down in his plush leather chair and shuffled through some papers.

"First, I will need you to read this letter very carefully and sign it. Then I can hand over the check, which you will see is already made out in your name. Although the amount is not exactly what you were asking for, it is a very large sum of money. I hope you are satisfied with this, Mr. Stanton. "

Thomas glanced at the check and without a word, began to read the letter, taking his time to be certain that he understood what it said. As Mr. Compton had informed him over the phone, the Church was prepared to compensate him on condition that he sign a release, relieving them from any further responsibility in the matter.

He continued reading. The release also stated that this was a one-time only and final payment, that the sum of money was never to be disclosed to any outside parties and that he, Thomas Paul Stanton, was sworn to absolute confidentiality in the matter.

Without hesitation and with a clear conscience, he signed his name on the document. He had done what he thought was best to bring Stumpf to justice, and with a desire that bordered on desperate, he needed to move on with his life.

He picked up the check and stood, ready to leave. Mr. Compton walked around his desk and offered his hand one last time. Thomas accepted it. Throughout his dealings with the Church, Thomas Paul sensed that the attorney had compassion for him, that Mr. Compton was a family man who didn't understand the gay lifestyle but felt fatherly towards Thomas nonetheless. Though his loyalty was to his employer, he seemed genuinely horrified at what Thomas had endured at the hands of the priest.

"Could I ask you one last question, Mr. Stanton?"

"Sure."

"Did you really write your letter to the Church on your own?"

"Yes, sir, that's correct." Thomas was aware that he had taken a big chance in attempting, without representation, to convince the Church to reckon with him. Perhaps his naiveté had worked in his favor. Regardless, it was miraculous that he had done it. Without spending a dime of his own money, excluding the paper and stamp, with no attorneys and no legal advice other than a few things Susan had shared with him, he had challenged them, and the truth had prevailed. He was proud of himself.

As Thomas exited the office, he folded the check in half and placed it in his shirt pocket.

Chapter 29

1992

Thomas, deep in thought, was reviewing his sketches of a house plan. He was not an architect and had never built a home but he was undaunted and had designed the house plans himself, gathering ideas from homes he had seen and admired around the city. The artist in him was adept at planning and drawing what would soon be his dream house. He was funding it with his settlement money from the Church. Determined not to squander it away on frivolous, unnecessary purchases, Thomas had decided early on that he would use the funds to procure for himself something that was important to him—the safety and security of a home.

His former home had sold over a year earlier, and he had taken Daniel with him to look for a new place to live. Thomas found a condo and fell in love with it. He was eager to move in but couldn't afford to live there on his own.

"Well, why don't you move in with me? We've been seeing each other for two years," Thomas said.

"Are you serious?" Daniel asked.

"Yes. I think we should make a go of our relationship."

Thomas heard the phone ring and moments later, Daniel called out to him.

"Your sister's on the phone."

"Thanks," Thomas called back as he picked up the kitchen extension. "Hello?"

"You'd better come. Its Mom." Anne Marie was distraught on the other end of the line.

Thomas rolled his eyes and sighed. "Not again. I can't do it." He was firm.

"But—"

He interrupted her. "No. This is already the third time this year that we've been summoned up there! She always does this, works herself into frenzy, almost overdosing because those damn doctors keep jacking her meds around, then claims she's dying and begs to be admitted."

Anne Marie interrupted him. "It's different this time. I know you've had issues with Mom lately. I understand. But you haven't been around in months.

"You don't know what's really going on." Her voice was cracking. "She's not the one saying she's dying this time—it's the doctors."

Thomas felt a lump swell in his throat.

"She's not at the nursing home anymore. She's been transferred to the ICU at Sacred Heart Hospital, and they've said she may only have a few hours left. She's been slipping in and out of consciousness all day." Anne Marie began to cry, and neither of them spoke for a moment. "She's dying, Thomas Paul. She needs to know that you love her before she goes. She's been asking for you." Thomas replaced the receiver and grabbed his keys off the kitchen counter.

As he drove to the hospital, he thought about his mother's last few years. He recalled confronting the doctors, finally, with his father's permission, about his mother's prescription-drug addiction. There had been years of futile pharmaceutical attempts, one after another, to try and stabilize her but none had succeeded. United as a family, they had insisted that she be taken off all non-life-saving medications. The withdrawal made it impossible for Anne Marie to continue caring for their mother at home, and they moved her into a nursing home, admitting her into their substance-abuse program. After weeks of anguish, for the first time in twenty years, Thomas Paul's family told him that his mother had at last found rest and stability.

He thought of the last time he had seen her—at Christmas. They had been together in the kitchen preparing dinner, but nothing he did was ever right. This time her constant demands had pushed him over the edge, and for the first time in his life, he had talked back to her.

"Mother, please! Either you just leave me alone and let me do it, or I'm not going to help anymore." His tone was firm.

His mother sighed. "Well, you know how sick I am, honey. If it's not prepared a certain way, I just can't eat it."

Thomas knew right then that he had lost his patience. He had spent his teenage years caring for her and he couldn't do it anymore. He realized he would never be able to do enough.

He had never been disrespectful to her and did not want to be but he knew her endless needs and demands would push him over the edge and he would snap. He had to figure out a way to find compassion and accept her for who she was, in hopes of having some sort of relationship with her. To do that, he needed to stay away for a while.

It was now March. Still unsure about how to re-enter her life, he had stayed away—never seeing her newfound peace. Now she was dying. Thomas pulled into the nearest parking space and hurried into the hospital.

He stood at the bedside and looked down at her frail frame. She was unrecognizable. After years of steroid use to combat her emphysema, her skin was paper-thin and jaundiced. Ravaged by years of drug use, she looked much older than her fifty-three years. Her mouth hung open and her breathing was labored.

Anne Marie stood on the other side of the bed and whispered into their mother's ear. "Mom, wake up. Mom." She kissed her translucent cheek. "Wake up, Mom Thomas Paul is here."

Thomas noticed his mother's eyes flutter open at the mention of his name. Their eyes made contact and he sensed some recognition in her distant stare. He hovered over her, looked directly in her eyes and began to cry. "I love you Mom. I'm so sorry I haven't been here for you."

After a moment, she reached up and gently waved him aside as if he were blocking her way out of the bed. As Thomas Paul took a step back, her breathing relaxed. The constant, raspy, gurgles of her long-diseased lungs were silent.

The rest of the family murmured to one another in hushed tones as Anne Marie and Thomas Paul stood vigil on either side of the bed. He watched her breathe. She seemed so restful. Her chest rose once again, she inhaled a deep breath and exhaled with the slow, peaceful ease of a newborn baby and then was still. Thomas Paul realized that she was gone.

The day of her funeral, the skies opened up and the rain poured down from morning until night. Thomas Paul could not contain his emotions. Daniel, steady, loving, and strong, supported him emotionally and physically when Thomas was certain his knees would buckle from inconsolable grief. He wasn't simply grieving for the mother who had left him. He was grieving for the mother he lost as a little boy.

As they lowered her into the ground, he choked on the heavy sobs of realization that with her coffin, there went his last chance of ever having the mother that he so desperately longed for. It had been an impossible fantasy in the back of his mind since he was a young boy. He had lived with that his whole life. But now that dream was buried beneath the heavy, wet, mounds of dirt. He would never again feel a loss this deep. The umbilical cord was severed.

With the support of his family, and Daniel's shoulder to lean on, Thomas was able to wade his way through the months of grief following his mother's death. He poured all his energy into the dream home that he would share with Daniel.

Daniel had become more to Thomas than even Susan had suspected. For the first time in his life, Thomas was in an adult, loving relationship.

If law would permit, they most certainly would have married.

Epilogue

Three Years Later

It was Sunday. Their flight for Italy was scheduled to leave in the late afternoon. It was their favorite thing to do together—travel. This was going to be their first trip to Europe. While Daniel stayed at home and finished packing, Thomas grabbed his bag and headed to the gym.

He pushed the door to the locker room open and spotted him. The priest. He had appeared at the gym weeks prior and Thomas had been shocked to see his shrunken, naked body emerging from the shower. His nakedness elicited a memory of repulsion.

No words were spoken. When Thomas looked him in the eye, Father Bob lowered his head and looked away.

That was the way it would be for years to come as they shared the same fitness facilities. Thomas questioned why fate would continue to put them in the same space every so often, but it didn't take him long to realize the answer. *These chance meetings are not for me—they are for him.* Each time was a reckoning, and Thomas Paul's forgiveness remained.

Across town, at St. Martins Church, Thomas' father reached out his hand and dropped his envelope in the collection plate.

About the Authors

ANDREA BOUVIER grew up in a small French-speaking town in Saskatchewan, Canada. Her love of literature and the English language was ignited by her tenth-grade English teacher. In 1992, she graduated with a degree in education from the University of Regina, Canada. Soon thereafter, she moved to Louisville, KY, and started a family.

With her two daughters well on their way, she reset her focus on her earlier passions and decided she wanted to write. Bouvier attended a writing workshop offered through the University of Louisville's Shelby Campus under the tutelage of a published author, the late Gary Devon. After completing the workshop, she joined a writer's group with some of her peers under the continued guidance of Mr. Devon and worked on her first, as yet unpublished, novel.

After years of sharing their mutual love of reading, Andrea and her close friend, Mark Clements, realized that they had a compelling and timely story to tell and believe they have done so with *Tall Trees*.

MARK RICHARD CLEMENTS is a practicing cosmetologist in Louisville. He derived most of his education informally, behind his chair. "Necessity is the mother of all invention," is a cliché with which Mark has come full circle.

Throughout his life, through necessity and invention, he has amassed a litany of skills and, as a result, has evolved as an artist. Channeling the awakened artist within, he has used words as brushstrokes on canvas, collaborating with his close friend, Andrea Bouvier, to tell this important story.

"All things are doable if the will to do so is there."

—*Mark Richard Clements*

Stay Connected

To stay connected with Mark and Andrea, visit their website and blog at www.talltreesnovel.com.

To learn where they will be appearing, signing books, or speaking, visit their events page at www.talltreesnovel.com.

To book Mark or Andrea for an event, contact them at markcandandreab@gmail.com.

www.ingramcontent.com/pod-product-compliance
Lightning Source LLC
Chambersburg PA
CBHW060540260626
47161CB00003B/978